I0544502

THE CARFAX INTRIGUE

TRACY GRANT

This book is licensed to you for your personal enjoyment only.

This is a work of fiction. Names, characters, places, and incidents are either products of the writer's imagination or are used fictitiously and are not to be construed as real. Any resemblance to actual events, locales, organizations, or persons, living or dead, is entirely coincidental.

The Carfax Intrigue
Copyright © 2020 by Tracy Grant

ISBN: 9781641972086
KDP POD ISBN: 9798559389363
IS POD ISBN: 9781641972093

ALL RIGHTS RESERVED.
No part of this work may be used, reproduced, or transmitted in any form or by any means, electronic or mechanical, without prior permission in writing from the publisher, except in the case of brief quotations embodied in critical articles or reviews.

NYLA Publishing
121 W 27th St., Suite 1201, New York, NY 10001
http://www.nyliterary.com

For all my friends in the performing arts who are finding ways to
create art or just survive
and all the theatres keeping a metaphorical ghost light on.

ACKNOWLEDGMENTS

My previous book, *The Tavistock Plot*, was finished at the beginning of the COVID-19 pandemic. *The Carfax Intrigue* was written entirely during the pandemic. As we navigate this uncertain time, I find myself more grateful than ever for the wonderful people who support me and my daughter and the Rannochs and their world in so many ways. As always, huge thanks to my wonderful agent, Nancy Yost, for her support and insights. Thanks to Natanya Wheeler for once again working her magic to create a cover that beautifully evokes Mélanie Rannoch and the Carfax House ballroom and for shepherding the book expertly through the publication process, to Sarah Younger for superlative social media support and for helping the book along through production and publication, and to the entire team at Nancy Yost Literary Agency for their fabulous work. Malcolm, Mélanie, and I are all very fortunate to have their support.

Thanks to Eve Lynch for the meticulous and thoughtful copyediting and to Kristen Loken for a magical author photo taken in one of my favorite places, San Francisco's War Memorial Opera House, on one of my favorite occasions of the year, the Merola Grand Finale. This photo is particularly poignant and precious now, with the lights dimmed in theatres and live performances canceled.

I am very fortunate to have a wonderful group of writer friends near and far who make being a writer less solitary. Thanks to Veronica Wolff and Lauren Willig, who both understand the challenges of being a writer and a mom. To Penelope Williamson, for sharing adventures, analyzing plots, and being a wonderful honorary aunt to my daughter. To Jami Alden, Tasha Alexander, Bella Andre, Allison Brennan, Josie Brown, Isobel Carr, Catherine Coulter, Deborah Coonts, Deborah Crombie, Carol Culver/Grace, Catherine Duthie, Alexandra Elliott, J.T. Ellison, Barbara Freethy, C.S. Harris, Candice Hern, Anne Mallory, Monica McCarty, Brenda Novak, Poppy Reifiin, Deanna Raybourn, and Jacqueline Yau.

Thank you to the readers who support Malcolm and Mélanie and their friends and provide wonderful insights on my Web site and social media.

Thanks to Gregory Paris and jim saliba for creating and updating a fabulous Web site that chronicles Malcolm and Mélanie's adventures. To Suzi Shoemake and Betty Strohecker for managing a wonderful Goodreads Discussion Group for readers of the series. Thanks to my colleagues at the Merola Opera Program who help me keep my life in balance—even on Zoom, I love spending time with you. And thanks to Mélanie herself, for inspiring my writing, being patient with Mummy's "work time", and offering her own insights at the keyboard. One of my proudest moments was when she said "Can I borrow your computer? I want to type the story I'm writing." This is Mélanie's contribution to this story – "My mommy is The best writer to me!!!!!!!!!!!!!!!!!!!!"

DRAMATIS PERSONAE

*indicates real historical figures

The Rannoch Family & Household

Mélanie Suzanne Rannoch, playwright and former French intelligence agent
Malcolm Rannoch, her husband, MP and former British intelligence agent
Colin Rannoch, their son
Jessica Rannoch, their daughter
Berowne, their cat

Laura O'Roarke, Colin and Jessica's former governess, teacher, and writer
Raoul O'Roarke, her husband, Mélanie's former spymaster, and Malcolm's father
Lady Emily Fitzwalter, Laura's daughter from her first marriage
Clara O'Roarke, Laura and Raoul's daughter

Gisèle Thirle, Malcolm's sister

Andrew Thirle, her husband

Miles Addison, Malcolm's valet
Blanca Mendoza Addison, his wife, Mélanie's companion
Pedro Addison, their son

The Davenport Family

Lady Cordelia Davenport, classicist
Colonel Harry Davenport, her husband, classicist, former
British intelligence agent
Livia Davenport, their daughter
Drusilla Davenport, their daughter

Archibald (Archie) Davenport, MP, Harry's uncle
Lady Frances Davenport, his wife, Malcolm's aunt
Francesca Davenport, their daughter
Philip Davenport, their son
Chloe Dacre-Hammond, Frances's daughter from her first
marriage

The Mallinson Family

Arthur (Julien St. Juste) Mallinson, Earl Carfax, former agent
for hire
Katelina (Kitty) Velasquez Mallinson, Countess Carfax, his wife,
former British and Spanish intelligence agent
Leo Ashford, her son
Timothy Ashford, her son
Guenevere (Genny) Ashford, Kitty and Julien's daughter

Hubert Mallinson, spymaster, Julien's uncle
Amelia Mallinson, his wife
Lucinda Mallinson, their youngest daughter

David Mallinson, MP, Hubert and Amelia's son

Simon Tanner, playwright, his lover

Mary Laclos, Hubert and Amelia's eldest daughter
Gui Laclos, her husband

Others

Bertrand Laclos, Gui's cousin, French émigré, former British intelligence agent
Rupert, Viscount Caruthers, his lover, MP, former British intelligence agent

Alexander (Sandy) Trenor
Elizabeth (Bet) Simcox, his mistress
Nan Simcox Lucan, her sister
Sam Lucan, Nan's husband
Helen Trenor, Lady Marchmain, Sandy's mother
Marcus Trenor, Lord Marchmain, Sandy's father

Kit Montagu, member of the Levellers
Sofia Montagu, his wife
Nerezza Russo, Sofia's friend
Benedict (Ben) Smythe, Nerezza's beau

Lord Beverston, member of the Elsinore League, Benedict's father
Sir George Dalton, Elsinore League member

William Barrington, Whig MP
Lord Wharton, Whig politician
Lady Harley, former mistress of Julien's father

Josefina Lopes Bennet, former agent and singer
Lucian Bennet, composer and violinist, her husband
Luisa Lopes, Josefina's mother

Fernando Lopes, Josefina's father

Edith Simmons, classicist and former governess who lives with
the Davenports
Alice, Lady Wilton, Edith's former employer
Thomas Thornsby, classicist
Lady Shroppington, Thomas's great-aunt, Elsinore League
member

Manon Caret Harleton, actress
Crispin, Lord Harleton, her husband

Jennifer Mansfield Smytheton, actress
Sir Horace Smytheton, her husband, former Elsinore League
member

James Fitzwalter, Duke of Trenchard, Laura's first husband's
brother

Lady Derby
Lord Derby, her husband

*Emily, Countess Cowper, patroness of Almack's
*Harry, Lord Palmerston, secretary at war, her lover

*Henry Brougham, MP, Queen Caroline's lawyer

Sylvie, Viscountess St. Ives, agent for hire

Jeremy Roth, Bow Street runner

Be as thou wast wont to be.
See as thou wast wont to see.
—Shakespeare, *A Midsummer Night's Dream,* Act IV, scene i

1

London
October 1820

ord Carfax adjusted a fold in his cravat. He'd been tying cravats without thinking about it for three decades, but for some reason tonight the linen had refused to cooperate. Which obviously had nothing to do with the state of his fingers. Because nerves were something he wouldn't admit to.

He tucked a fold under his gray silk waistcoat, though it should have been perfect before he put the waistcoat on. The damned candles on either side of the looking glass kept flickering, which didn't help. Perhaps he should light a lamp.

"Aren't you ready, darling?" His wife appeared in the dressing room doorway, fastening a pearl bracelet he'd given her round her wrist. "It's less than half an hour until the guests are due to arrive."

"This is Mayfair, my sweet. They'll be fashionably late."

"Someone's sure to be early in hopes of gleaning information. Or simply to catch us off our guard."

"You have a point." He stuck his diamond stickpin into the

cravat. At a rather awkward angle. Oh, well. He'd start making a practice of it and set a new fashion. He reached for his coat. Tailored on Bond Street, as nearly all his coats had been even when he'd lived in exile. "I'm never going to look at myself and see Lord Carfax."

"I should hope not." Kitty came up behind him and smoothed her hands over the black superfine shoulders of the coat. "I don't want to wonder what's become of the man I married. Besides, it's what other people see that matters. And you've always been very good at making other people see precisely what you want them to."

He turned and caught her hands in his own. She was wearing apricot gauze draped with an artistry befitting Aphrodite over a matching satin slip. Her tawny hair was piled high with curls escaping an antique gold bandeau to fall about her face. The pearl bracelet was round her wrist, citrines from her native Spain were at her ears and round her throat, and the emerald ring he'd given her when they married was on her hand. "You look beautiful."

"I feel like an imposter. Which is odd considering how much of my life I've spent playing a role. And this role is actually the truth."

"Truth can be damnably hard to play, as I'm sure Manon and Letty and Will and our other actor friends would confirm."

She leaned in and kissed him, lightly, but she clung for a moment. He tightened his arms round her—carefully so as not to disturb her gown. She drew back and gave a rueful smile. "Oh dear. I've got lip rouge on you."

"Never mind." He smoothed it off, but not quite completely. "It will give them something to gossip about."

"Because they'll think it's mine or someone else's?"

"Either way. But probably more if they think it's yours."

"Good. Nothing like a touch of scandal to lend interest. And it may stop people from talking about other things."

He lifted her hands to his lips, each in turn. "You didn't wear the Carfax rubies."

"Strategic choice. I'm going to be my sort of Lady Carfax."

"My darling Kitkat. You're always going to be your own anything." He picked up his gloves and held out his arm. She slid her own through it. They stopped in the nursery where Leo and Timothy made them repeat their promises to bring up ices and cakes, and Genny added a sticky print on his cravat to the smear of lip rouge. He'd always been known for his immaculate linen, but he decided to leave it for good luck.

They heard voices in the hall as they went downstairs. Mélanie and Malcolm Rannoch, and Raoul and Laura O'Roarke, who had all been an invaluable support these past months. He'd known Malcolm Rannoch since they were boys. He'd worked with Mélanie on more than one mission, notably when they helped the Empress Josephine's daughter Hortense conceal a secret pregnancy (he'd also spent one memorable night with her, but that was hardly something to dwell on now when she was more a friend than anything). He'd worked with and against O'Roarke for a quarter century and learned far more from him than he'd ever admit. He'd known Laura the least of all of them, but had grown very fond of her, as well as having a great deal of respect for her skills. And the Rannochs and O'Roarkes had brought another couple with them as well. As Julien descended the stairs, he saw the tall figure of Andrew Thirle, Malcolm Rannoch's brother-in-law, and beside him, half hidden behind Malcolm, whom she was talking to, Malcolm's younger sister Gisèle Thirle. Whom Julien had started training to be an agent when she was fourteen. And who was now one of the most formidable agents he knew. Even by the very impressive standards of the group gathered in the Carfax House hall.

"I'm so glad you're all here early." Kitty smiled as they went down the rest of the steps.

"We thought you could use the moral support," Mélanie said.

"And the practical support," Kitty said. "Come into the supper room and see how things look."

"I can offer the rest of you a drink," Julien said. "I imagine we could all do with the fortification."

In the library, he poured whisky for all of them and marveled both at the oddity of having friends and of welcoming them to the house he had grown up in but until recently hadn't ever thought to return to. Very often this group gathered in the midst of an investigation, but tonight the mood was surprisingly carefree. Until he put a glass into Gisèle's hand, and Gisèle's fingers tightened round his arm. "Could we have a word in private?"

Julien met her gaze, then nodded. A few moments later, after they had made their excuses to the others, none of whom, including Gisèle's husband, seemed particularly surprised, they removed to the study.

Gisèle took a sip from her glass and regarded him across the room that had once been the sanctum of his uncle, Hubert Mallinson, who had been Lord Carfax for the quarter century Julien had been presumed dead. And who was also Gisèle's father, though Gisèle hadn't known it until recently.

Gisèle set her glass down and smiled at him. "You don't look different."

"I should hope not. I'm the same person."

She moved to one of the chairs in front of the desk. Julien had replaced the straight-backed chairs Carfax used for his guests with a pair of cushioned armchairs designed for friendly chats. "Ought I to start calling you Arthur?"

"Not if you expect me to answer." Julien dropped into the chair opposite her instead of the one behind the desk. He'd kept his uncle's desk because it was practical and contained all sorts of hidden compartments worthy of a spymaster, but it still didn't feel like his. Despite his and Kitty's having gone to considerable lengths to make it their own.

"I haven't been Arthur for more than half my life. And it never suited me."

Gisèle took another sip of whisky. "Arthur was Britain's savior."

"Yes, there's always been more than a touch of irony in the name. Even when I was a boy."

Gisèle set her glass on the table between the chairs. "I think it suits you." She regarded him for a moment. "Andrew and I came down from Scotland to be here tonight. Well, and to see the family. We were going to just come and enjoy the ball. But I received information this afternoon."

"I thought perhaps you did." Julien took a drink of whisky. "It's a bit of a relief. I'd much rather be an agent than an earl just now."

"Being an earl could be excellent cover for being an agent." Gisèle learned forwards. Her honey blonde hair was pinned up with cropped ringlets falling about her face, not streaming down her back, and it was held with pearl combs, not a pink hair ribbon, but she had the same intent expression she had worn from the time she was fourteen when they discussed a mission. "The League have got hold of papers. Letters, I think, that could have a bearing on the case against Queen Caroline."

Caroline of Brunswick, estranged wife of the former prince regent, who had become George IV on the death of his father at the end of the previous January, had recently returned to Britain after several years of living in Italy. She was now queen consort, though neither she nor her husband had been crowned. Her husband, who had been unhappy with the match from the start, was attempting to push a divorce through the House of Lords. Of which Julien was now a member. And the Elsinore League, a shadowy organization of powerful men in Britain and abroad dedicated to promoting their own interests, had been the target of Gisèle's mother and through her of Julien and Gisèle and the Rannochs and their friends. Gisèle had been working undercover with them for a year and a half.

"Damnation," Julien said. "Given how much the League have been operating in Italy, I should have suspected that. Don't tell me they're letters the queen wrote? Or Bergami?" Bergami was Queen Caroline's courier and—many claimed (probably with accuracy)—her lover.

"No." Gisèle smoothed her hands over her skirt. "I don't know all the details, but apparently they were written by an English lady abroad who was friends with the queen."

"And she reported salacious secrets the queen confided to her?"

"Not precisely. I gather the letters might help either side, depending on which parts of them were used. Though overall they seem to actually support the queen's cause rather than hurt it."

"Well, that's interesting." Julien sat back in his chair. "I'd rather have thought the League would support the king if they took sides."

"The League seem to be interested in what is most to their advantage. As usual. They're offering to sell the papers to the highest bidder."

Julien set his glass down beside Gisèle's. "Let me guess. Someone is buying them at the ball tonight?"

"Being an earl hasn't blunted your edge."

"Kitty wouldn't let that happen. So is Henry Brougham or Thomas Denman or some of the Radicals or Whigs who support the queen buying the papers to bolster her cause?" Brougham and Denman were the queen's lawyers.

"No." Gisèle reached for her glass but tightened her fingers round it instead of taking a drink. "They were outbid, it seems. If they were the buyers, I'd rather be inclined to leave the whole thing alone." She watched him for a moment. "Wouldn't you?"

"Support a neglected wife whose husband has philandered

quite as much as she has, kept her daughter from her, and generally ill used her? Can you doubt it?" Julien reached for his glass and tossed down a sip. "Aside from the fact that I took my seat in Parliament as a Whig."

"And your maiden speech has you branded a Radical." Gisèle took a drink from her own glass.

"Mmm." Julien twisted his glass between his fingers. "I do like to shake things up. Who's buying the papers tonight, Gelly?"

Gisèle set down her glass. "Carfax. That is, the former Lord Carfax."

Julien clunked his glass down beside Gisèle's. "I might have known it. If anyone knows how to conduct secret meetings in this house, he certainly does."

"The things is, Carfax—your Uncle Hubert—what the devil am I supposed to call him? If I say Mallinson, it sounds like I mean David."

Julien sank further back in his chair. "You could always call him Father."

"No." Gisèle's fingers curved round the arms of her chair. "For any number of reasons."

"Better call him Hubert, then. Or if you need to be more formal in public, Colonel Mallinson. He was a lieutenant colonel when he became earl and left the military. Are you asking me to intercept the papers?"

"I'm sorry. I know how important tonight is for you and Kitty—"

Julien gave a whoop of laughter. "My darling Gelly. Can you know me so little you can think I wouldn't relish the distraction of a mission on this of all nights?"

"Well, when you put it that way—no." Gisèle grinned. For a moment she was the brilliant, lonely fourteen-year-old he'd met in the caves beneath Dunmykel, the Rannochs' Scottish estate.

Julien returned her smile. "We should tell Malcolm and

Mélanie and the O'Roarkes. And Andrew. Probably the Davenports too. We could use their help."

Gisèle's brows drew together.

"Surely you don't think they won't all want to help," Julien said.

"No, of course not. But—"

"Trying to do everything on your own can be dangerous. I tried to teach you that, though I don't think I always set the best example."

"It's not that. If Malcolm gets too close to—"

Julien watched her steadily. "We're going to have to tell him, Gelly. Not just this. All of it."

"No!"

"Or he's going to work it out for himself. He did about me."

"That was different." Gisèle's fingers locked tight together. "This—"

"We're going to need his help." Julien leaned forwards. "And there could be more damage if he finds out the wrong way."

Gisèle folded her arms over her chest in a gesture that made her look very like Malcolm. "I was afraid of this. You and Malcolm have got to be friends and now you're not being sensible about the whole situation."

"That's a matter of perspective. I'd say I'm more aware of the damage we're doing. We can't contain this, Gelly. And I speak as one used to containing things."

"You think I don't know how hard it is to keep the secret? I keep it from Andrew every day—" She broke off and studied Julien, her gaze sharpening.

"No, I haven't told Kitty. We've both always known we were going to have secrets from each other. Though I'll confess, since Kitty and I've married—since we became a couple—I understand better what you've been going through with Andrew."

"It's not easy," Gisèle said. "But it's necessary."

"It was. Or it seemed to be." Julien let his gaze settle on her own. He was still conscious of an impulse to protect her, but she deserved to be treated like an equal. "The game is changing. We're going to need all of them. And if Malcolm learns from someone else, it could be worse."

Gisèle shifted in her chair. "We don't need to tell them about it to retrieve the papers."

"No. That debate can wait. But we're going to need the whole team tonight."

"Since when do you talk about teams?"

Julien pushed himself to his feet. "I may not be Arthur, but I'm not the man I was."

2

Kitty tugged at her gloves and ran her gaze over the long central supper table and the smaller dining tables scattered about it. The footmen—Kitty and Julien's own and the carefully vetted additions they had hired for the evening—had just lit the wax tapers. The light gleamed on the silver and the freshly pressed damask of the table linens. "I hope we have enough champagne."

Mélanie smiled. Kitty was nervous tonight in a way Mélanie had never seen before. They'd known each other less than a year, but they'd shared some particularly harrowing experiences in that time, and Kitty had shown herself imperturbable. "There was one particularly warm night when Valentin told me we were on our last case of champagne while I was still at the head of the stairs greeting the guests."

Kitty's fingers froze on the silk of her gloves. "What did you do?"

"Asked Valentin to find Lady Frances and Cordy. They both sent home and had more champagne delivered. We can easily send to Berkeley Square tonight if you happen to need it. And Frances and Cordy will help as well."

Kitty adjusted one of the roses in the bouquet at the center of the supper table. "We're fortunate in our friends. It's the things going wrong I haven't thought of that concern me."

"Yes, there's always that." Mélanie tugged one of the gathered puffed sleeves of her gown into place. She had ordered the gown, a tawny gold silk with little adornment but an extravagant sweeping skirt, when she took Kitty to her modiste, Marthe Leblanc. "But then, improvisation is part of the challenge of a mission. And the fun."

Kitty turned from adjusting the flowers and gave a crooked smile. "I've gone undercover knowing I was likely to be shot if I was caught. I've been in skirmishes. I've been wounded. I've played a host of roles. I don't know why this one is bothering me so much."

"The beau monde will do that to you. Besides, you'd been going into danger since you were young. This is uncharted territory. At least, that's how it was for me when I married Malcolm."

"Being married to Edward should have prepared me. That was odd enough. Being an officer's wife. Getting used to the expectations and the rules that I suppose aren't any odder than the ones I grew up with, just—different. In some ways, at least. But the scale was smaller than"—she glanced round the long room, the Ionic columns, the classical busts set in niches, the French windows framed in gilded wrought iron leading to a balcony that overlooked the garden, the chandelier hung from an intricate plaster medallion, its crystals sparkling in the candlelight—"than this."

Mélanie pushed a vase a half-inch over on its table. "To be honest, when we first came to Britain and I realized the scale of the world Malcolm had been born to, I was shocked. But you haven't any need to care what any of them thinks of you. Just because you're Lady Carfax doesn't mean you can't be whoever you want. In fact, it gives you more freedom in a way. Unless, of course, you want a position in the beau monde."

Kitty laughed. "Can you imagine I would?"

"For yourself?" Mélanie studied the woman who had been Malcolm's first love, who was now her own friend. A better friend than she would have thought possible when they met. But there was still a great deal about Kitty she did not know. "It's hard to fathom. You might want what it could bring you."

"I'll confess I'm not immune to the advantages of being able to wield influence for Spain." Kitty adjusted the angle of one of the supper chairs. Like Raoul, she was deeply committed to the liberals in Spain rebelling against the restored Bourbon monarchy. "On the other hand, if I want to accomplish what I'd like to, I'm unlikely to be fully accepted."

"That rather depends on how much your goal is known. Though having a goal does make this world harder to navigate." Mélanie reached up to push a pin more firmly into her hair. It felt odd to be wearing it pinned into an elaborate knot instead of just pulling the front back and leaving the rest tumbling loose, as she'd taken to wearing it. "I never precisely had that."

"Mélanie, darling." Kitty turned from angling another chair. "As I understand it, when you married Malcolm you had a very clear goal indeed."

Mélanie met her friend's gaze. They had never really talked about how she had gone into her own marriage in order to spy on Malcolm. She wasn't even precisely sure how Kitty had learned the truth, though she assumed it had come from Julien. Kitty, who had been Malcolm's lover and on the opposite side from Mélanie in the Peninsular War, could be pardoned for having a less than charitable view of her behavior.

Kitty gave a quick smile. "I can't tell you how much I admire your daring. It must have been fiendishly uncomfortable. "

Mélanie kept her gaze steady. "It was."

Kitty tilted her head, her side curls stirring her citrine

earrings. "I'd have probably done the same, if the opportunity had offered. Before I had children. Though I doubt it would have worked out so well. Oh, don't think I don't feel a qualm for Malcolm. But that's the risk we all accept as agents, isn't it?"

A tumult of feelings that would never completely go away squeezed Mélanie's chest, like the unfamiliar laces of the corset she was wearing tonight. "So I told myself."

"So, I'm quite sure, Malcolm tells himself."

"Malcolm is a master at understanding." So much so that she could believe, at times, that the divide between them was as easily repaired as Malcolm pretended it was.

"So he is. Though, oddly, I think he understood your actions better than mine. I assume he's told you about that—Don Ramón Castella's son."

Mélanie nodded. Kitty had wanted to turn the guerrillero's *afrancesado* son over to the former Lord Carfax, their spymaster at the time. Kitty had seen it as one more step in pushing for the Spain she wanted—a liberal Spain, but with the French driven out. Malcolm had seen it as a betrayal of trust. "I'm not sure what I'd have done in your place."

"I'm not sure what I'd do if I faced the decision again," Kitty said. "I wouldn't say I've softened, but being a mother I'd be more inclined to realize I was dealing with someone's son, I think. Or simply that it was the life of another human being."

She had never, Mélanie realized, spoken with someone who could understand her past actions on quite this level. "You said you might have done what I did. If someone else had done it to you, could you have forgiven them?"

Kitty gave a rueful, thoughtful smile. "I'm not sure. I don't like being outwitted. To own the truth, that was more than half the reason I got so angry with Malcolm when he went round me and warned Don Ramón's son. I saw it as being outwitted. He saw it as saving a life. Which I didn't properly appreciate until years later." She looked at Mélanie for a moment, her gaze at once warm and level. "Could you have forgiven Malcolm if your situations were reversed?"

Mélanie drew in a breath and felt her corset laces bite into her skin. "I've asked myself that a hundred times. I don't know. I'd have understood. I think I'm honest enough for that. I'm not sure about forgiving—I might have been too busy blaming myself."

"A sad waste of time."

"That's what Raoul says. But he does it as much as any of us."

"Oh, possibly more so. He's ruthlessly hard on himself. He's just better than most of us at concealing it." Kitty smoothed a wrinkle from her glove. "Perhaps the real question isn't if one can forgive, but if one wants to go on."

"That sounds like something Malcolm might say."

"And it's quite clear he wants to go on." Kitty was silent again, as though choosing her words with care, or perhaps uncertain about whether to speak at all. "I said I'd probably have done what you did, married a man to spy on him, and that I wasn't sure I could forgive a man who did the same to me. But I'm quite sure I couldn't do what you did later—give up my cause and stay in my marriage."

For a moment Mélanie felt as though her satin slippers were rooted to the polished floorboards. "I didn't give it up for a long time."

"But you did in the end."

Which had ended a conflict that had been tearing her in two. And yet, at the same time it had left a hollow void inside her. Not that she hadn't worked for what she believed in after she stopped spying, but mostly she hadn't done it on her own; she'd done it with Malcolm, largely in her role as a diplomatic and political wife. "We couldn't have gone on if I hadn't. Malcolm couldn't have lived with me, and I couldn't have lived with myself. And I love what we do together. But I did need something that was my own."

"And now you have your writing."

Which meant more to her than she could possibly say. Her first play that had premiered last January, the new one she was currently finishing. And God knows she put her ideas in her plays, ideas she'd been formulating for years. But she was a bit surprised that Kitty, so on the edge of trying to bring about change, understood that. Mélanie nodded, choosing her words carefully. "It means a lot to have my own voice." She hesitated a moment, but Kitty was struggling with many of the things she had struggled with, so it seemed important to speak. "For a long time, I thought I had to do it all perfectly. Host parties. Accept the right invitations. Charm the right people. At first, to be brutally honest, it was because the better situated we were, the more I was accepted as the perfect wife, the better I could gather information. But I also thought Malcolm deserved that much. Deserved a wife who was at least an asset in all those public ways. Then I thought I needed to make the past up to him in some way. He never told me he wanted a beau monde wife, but he was part of the beau monde, so it seemed we had to fit into that world. It took running off to exile in Italy for us both to realize we didn't care. Even now, I juggle how much I need to play the game."

"I told Julien at the start that I wouldn't give up my work. Not that he'd want me to. But I suppose—" Kitty looked down at her glove and smoothed another wrinkle from it. "I want Julien to be able to make what he wishes of being Lord Carfax. I don't want my being his wife to stand in his way." She looked up and caught Mélanie's gaze. "Don't you dare ever tell him I said that."

"I wouldn't dream of it. Though I very much doubt Julien wants to be a conventional Lord Carfax. And I'm quite sure he'd be horrified by the thought of your being anything but who you want to be."

"That's precisely why I don't want you to tell him. And, of course, he doesn't want to be conventional. But—" Kitty glanced at a portrait of a sixteenth-century Mallinson that hung between two of the niches with classical busts. "It's his world. It's one thing for him to choose not to engage with it, but I don't want him to be pushed out or to feel he needs to remove himself. He can do a lot and still be Lord Carfax. He doesn't say it in so many words, but I know he's worried about my being like his mother. I don't want that to hold him back. Because of course, I'm not Pamela Carfax. I married my husband because I love him, not because I was pushed into an arranged marriage, and I'm four-and-thirty, not seventeen. I won't let myself be swallowed up by this. But I want him to have the life he wants."

"I said that about Malcolm for years. But my case was a bit different. I felt I had a lot to make up to him for. Which I certainly did. But one partner's trying to make up to the other for the past is a poor foundation for a marriage. Which it took me a while to see."

"Don't tell me you've stopped worrying about making Malcolm happy."

"No, of course not. After all, that's part of what being a couple means."

"But you don't want to let him see it."

Mélanie moved her fingers over the sticks of her fan, painted with a scene from *Le nozze di Figaro*. Malcolm had given it to her when they were at the Congress of Vienna, both of them caught up in the intricate diplomatic game, both of them keeping secrets that strained their marriage to the breaking point. "If he saw it, he'd worry."

Kitty's mouth curved in a smile. "Precisely. I complain when Julien fusses over me, so I can understand he'd feel the same about being fussed over."

"Yes, I can quite imagine it. Of course, looking at the guest list for tonight, I'd say Julien isn't the least worried about fitting in."

"There is that." Kitty twisted the emerald ring Julien had

given her beneath her glove. "It's an odd thing, caring so much for someone else's happiness. I haven't before."

"You care for your children's."

"Well, of course; that's different."

"Not everyone does." Mélanie hesitated, wondering if she should say it. "And I think you cared for Malcolm's. More than you ever let him realize."

Kitty gave a quick smile. "A good thing for all of us that I did. We're all much happier as we are. And I'll own I've rebelled against the idea I should be nurturing."

Mélanie gave a sigh of understanding. "I know precisely what you mean."

"Though I will admit it can be rather agreeable to be fussed over on occasion. Don't let Julien hear I said that either." Kitty made a last adjustment to the roses. "There. It's always the hardest thing on a mission, or preparing for a ball. Knowing when to stop tweaking." She looked over her shoulder as Cordelia Davenport stepped into the room, her gown of figured ivory gauze over primrose satin catching the candlelight. The three of them had coordinated their gowns to go with the gilding in Carfax House and the peach roses they'd chosen for the ball.

"I'm so glad you're here," Kitty said, going forwards with a smile. "You can confirm if it looks all right."

"It looks splendid," Cordelia said. "Even better than what we envisioned. The ball is going to be a triumph."

"I'll be very happy if we just get through it. Should I go to the head of the stairs?"

"Not just yet. Julien asked me to see if you could both come to the library." Cordy looked between Kitty and Mélanie. "Apparently he and Gelly have something to tell us."

~

Silence hung over the library when Julien and Gisèle finished explaining about the letters the former Lord Carfax planned to buy from the Elsinore League at the ball.

"I should have known it," Malcolm said. "Carfax—Hubert—has seemed much too agreeable lately."

"Who's giving him the papers?" Raoul asked. He was leaning forwards on the sofa, hands clasped, face intent.

"Sir George Dalton," Gisèle said.

Looks shot among the group. Dalton was a minor Tory politician. Mélanie had been seated next to him at the Castlereaghs' once and had danced with him a few times in the days when they went out in society more.

"We knew he was a League member," Malcolm said. "From the lists we recovered in Italy. But hardly one of the leaders. Which I suppose makes him well situated to handle the papers. They'd think he wouldn't be suspected."

"Which faction in the League is selling the papers?" Mélanie asked. "The main one or the one trying to wrest control?"

"The one trying to wrest control," Gisèle said. "Assuming I understand correctly."

"Easier to get the papers before Carfax receives them," Mélanie said. "I mean Colonel Mallinson. Hubert. I'm never going to get used to this."

"My thoughts exactly," Malcolm said. "On both counts."

"No argument," Julien said. "Though I'd quite welcome the challenge of trying to get the letters away from Uncle Hubert."

"We have enough challenges tonight." Kitty reached for his hand. They were sitting side by side on a blue velvet settee. Mélanie could remember the former Lord and Lady Carfax sitting on that same settee, though not their ever holding hands. Or plotting a mission.

"Don't worry, my sweet." Julien lifted Kitty's gloved hand to his lips. "I've become positively prudent."

"Ha." Kitty tucked her arm through his. "I think Mélanie would have the best chance getting the papers."

"The League will be on guard with me," Mélanie said. "But then, that's true of all of us. Laura might do better—she managed to steal a paper from Carfax. The former Carfax."

"And he probably knows I did it by now," Laura said.

"We need to divert Carfax—Hubert—while one of you gets the papers," Malcolm said.

"Julien and I can help with the diversion," Kitty said. "Sadly, I don't think we can help with retrieving the papers."

"No, all eyes will be on you both tonight," Mélanie said. "You can help by distracting everyone. Fortunately, they'll be busy looking at you."

"Decoy's not my favorite role on a mission," Kitty said, "but we'll manage."

Julien scraped the toe of his polished shoe over the Axminster carpet. "I don't suppose—"

"No," Malcolm, Mélanie, and Raoul said in unison.

"You have a point. And I was just telling Gelly about the value of teamwork. I need to do better at following my own advice. I expect all this is making me a better parent. Not to mention a better person. I wouldn't have thought I'd admit to that mattering. Still—"

"Do stop piffling on, darling." Kitty gripped his arm. "We have work to do."

"I could—" Gisèle began.

"No." This time it was Malcolm and Julien who spoke in unison.

"You can't be anywhere near Dalton or Uncle Hubert or any of this, Gelly," Julien said. "Or you'll destroy the credit you've managed to keep with the League."

Gisèle nodded reluctantly. "So there's no role for me."

"On the contrary," Malcolm said. "You can look completely natural and as though you're doing nothing but enjoying the ball with Andrew. Believe me, it's one of the hardest roles on a mission. Not least because one feels sidelined."

Gisèle grimaced but nodded.

Andrew reached for her hand. "At least in this I can help."

Gisèle gave a quick smile and squeezed his fingers.

Cordelia's husband Harry was staring into his whisky glass with the look of one scouting terrain. "I don't suppose we could bash Dalton over the head? Like we did to get the Darlington letters?"

"Not a bad idea," Malcolm said. "I think we are going to need to knock him out. But something subtler is called for. Kitty, I hope you have a spare footman's uniform about."

"Certainly," Kitty said, "but even in the guise of a footman, any of us is likely to be recognized. More to the point, we'll draw suspicion if we aren't in the ballroom."

"Quite. That's why it's a very good thing Addison and Blanca will be here shortly."

Julien had been very insistent on inviting Addison, Malcolm's valet, and Blanca, Mélanie's companion, both also fellow agents, to the ball. He'd been very insistent on including a number of people, but Addison and Blanca had been among the most difficult to persuade to attend. Addison, far more a conventional valet than Blanca had ever been a conventional lady's maid, was very careful to preserve the lines of master and servant. At least, he had been when Mélanie first met him. He had unbent remarkably in the intervening years. He even dined with them at times when it was just the family or the family and a few guests, and would go to casual parties at the homes of close friends like the Davenports. But attending a Mayfair ball was something very different. Finally, Blanca had said that it would be an insult to Kitty and Julien not to go and they deserved all the support they could get from their friends. And Addison, who was as kind and as good a friend as he was conscious of the forms, had relented.

"Excellent," Harry said. "Very good you invited them, Julien."

"That wasn't why," Julien said. "Though their talents always make them an asset to have about."

"Do you always think about having guests who are intelligence assets?" Andrew asked with genuine curiosity. Julien, so close to Gisèle, still appeared to be something of a mystery to Gisèle's husband.

"I wouldn't say I'm accustomed to having guests at all," Julien said. "One has to have a home to have guests, and I've never really had a home. But any large gathering is potentially a mission. That's the way I've lived my life. And I don't see it changing."

"Not with the League to deal with," Cordelia said. "Not to mention the king and queen's divorce." She frowned. "I suppose we should have known the League would get tangled up in the divorce. And try to turn it to their advantage."

"Or, evidently, their profit," Raoul said.

Gisèle nodded. "I think they'd be inclined to side with the king, but mostly they're hoping to turn the spectacle to their advantage."

"Which gives them something in common with about ninety percent of those who'll be present tonight," Malcolm said. "It should be an interesting evening."

3

---

*J*ulien paused beside Mélanie on the edge of the dance floor, where she had been scanning the growing crowd under cover of adjusting the clasp on her gold-and-garnet bracelet. "Dalton hasn't arrived yet, as far as I can tell."

"No, believe me, I'm watching carefully." Mélanie pushed the bracelet in place on her gloved wrist and took the champagne glass he was holding out. "Raoul and Laura are in the supper room, Harry's in the card room with Archie, whom he's enlisted, and Malcolm and Cordy are somewhere about the ballroom. I must say, it's agreeable to have a mission."

"Mmm. While I'm left to play the host." Julien cast a glance towards the open doors to the stairhead. "Kitty seems to have things in hand greeting the guests. I'd like to help, but not much I can do."

Mélanie smiled. "There are times when husbands are superfluous."

Julien grinned. "Only times?"

Mélanie touched her glass to his. "They have their uses."

"You're quite forbearing."

"About what?"

He took a sip from his own glass. "Not throwing it in my teeth what I've become."

Mélanie regarded the man whom Raoul, hardly a man one would call safe, had described as the most dangerous agent on the Continent, when she first met him. "What? A British aristocrat? A husband? A father? A Radical politician?"

"All of them," Julien said.

"You never claimed not to be an aristocrat," Mélanie said. "You always rather had the air of one."

"Don't tell me you think that's something one is born with."

"Not born, but bred. And you grew up as an aristocrat for almost sixteen years. Then, on our journey with Hortense you admitted you could feel the allure of a home and family. When I still scoffed at the very idea."

"Yes, I should have remembered I'd said that when I later marveled at your domesticity. Perhaps you read my envy even then."

"You've never been envious in your life, Julien."

"So you say, *cara*. But then, I've always had something of a knack for hiding my feelings."

"Along with a talent for massive understatement." Even two years ago, after she'd worked with him and relied on him on that mission with Hortense, she'd been terrified when he'd arrived in Britain, close to the safe world of her family. And yet—"But I wasn't quite so surprised to see you as a husband and father as you might think. Now, when it comes to being a Radical politician—you did rather have me convinced you didn't believe in anything."

Julien leaned against a column and took another sip of champagne. "Cynicism's a convenient pose. And not nearly as much work as your and O'Roarke's tiresome ideals. But there is something to be said for making oneself useful."

Mélanie fixed him with the gaze she gave her children when they were prevaricating. "You're a fraud, Julien."

He gave her a sidelong smile. "You've only just realized that?"

"I've had a glimmering for a while. But not as much with you as with others." Such as her former spymaster Raoul. Even he had kept his mask up for a very long time. And she had failed to see behind it far longer than she should have done.

"Survival technique. And a way not to disappoint people. Including myself."

Mélanie glanced through the open double doors to the head of the stairs. The crowd entering the ballroom thinned for a moment and she could see Kitty holding out her hand to a man with the distinctive hooked-nose profile of the Duke of Wellington.

"Kitty makes it look easy," she said.

"Yes. Easier than it is, I think." Julien's eyes narrowed.

"There are ways being a beau monde hostess can be fun. As long as one doesn't feel trapped in it. I don't think Kitty remotely feels trapped."

"I hope to God not." Julien's tone wasn't quite as mocking as usual.

"Even I never did."

Julien shot a look at her. "No?"

"Well, not precisely." Scenes from her past shot through Mélanie's mind. The first party she'd given in Lisbon as Malcolm's bride, the first time she'd acted as hostess for the ambassador, Sir Charles Stuart. Parties and elaborate social events in Vienna at the Congress, in Brussels on the eve of Waterloo, in Paris. Each time stepping onto a new stage. Precarious but exhilarating. After all, she had grown up in the theatre. She enjoyed trying out new roles. "But I was pretending."

"We're all pretending, to a degree." Julien's voice softened in that disconcerting way it sometimes could. "Hopefully less with the people we love than with others. But one likes to avoid placing undue burdens on anyone. And hopefully Kitty will never see the truth."

"The truth about what?" Mélanie asked.

Julien gave a twisted smile. "How very desperately her happiness matters to me."

MALCOLM MOVED along the edge of the dance floor, one eye out for Sir George Dalton. He saw Gisèle waltzing with Andrew, giving a very good impression of doing nothing but enjoying a night out with her husband, and then stopped short at the sight of his friend David Mallinson, Julien's cousin. Who had grown up in this house. Malcolm could keenly remember the way becoming Viscount Worsley, on the death of his uncle shortly following Julien's supposed death, had seemed to almost physically weigh David down. Now David was David Mallinson again. The smile he greeted Malcolm with had his usual reserve, but also seemed easier than it had in years. Perhaps since they were children.

"It seems to be going splendidly," David said. "Kitty looks very at ease. I love what she's done with the house."

Malcolm knew how glad David was to have found Julien again, for a number of reasons. Still, it couldn't but be odd to be a guest in the house he had grown up in and to see his parents as guests. "It must be a bit strange being here."

"Less nerve-wracking. Mother's not throwing eligible girls at me. No need to play the host, just a minor cousin."

"Hardly minor."

"Julien has things well in hand. And once everyone gets accustomed to the fact that I don't mind, it will be even easier. I've been getting a lot of sidelong looks and people so pointedly not commenting on the situation it's a comment in and of itself. Truth to tell, that's been happening every time I've gone out in company ever since Julien's—Arthur's—return became public. It's enough to make one a recluse. If I didn't—Good God. Is that Sam Lucan?"

Malcolm glanced across the room. Sam Lucan and his wife Nan were near the door talking to Mélanie and Cordelia. Sam had been an agent in the Peninsula, supplying guns to the French and their allies and sometimes to the British as well. Mélanie had helped him settle in London after the war, in the days when Malcolm hadn't known the truth of her past. Sam had been engaged in some questionable activities in St. Giles, about which, Malcolm thought, the less he knew the better as an MP. But in the past year Sam had married Nan and settled in new lodgings Malcolm had helped them find. "Yes, he's an old friend of Julien's."

"I know. I just—didn't expect to see him here."

Malcolm turned his gaze back to David. "You've seen him in Berkeley Square more than once."

"That's different. I mean, it wasn't this sort of a ball." David shifted his weight from one foot to the other. "With Father and Mother present."

"He was at Raoul and Laura's wedding. Along with your parents."

"I know, but that was—I'm not trying to be stuffy. I'm just—"

"Used to the forms." There was a certain unwritten code to a Mayfair ball. Which Malcolm and Mélanie had cheerfully broken with some time ago.

"No. Maybe. A bit. The wedding didn't surprise me so much. That was O'Roarke."

"This is Julien."

"Yes, in that sense it's very like Julien. But I'm not sure—Is he generally including his friends from all different parts of his life, or stirring up mischief, or making a statement—or does he have some other goal in mind?"

"You'll have to ask him."

David looked across the room at Julien, then shot his gaze back to Malcolm. "He didn't invite Billy, did he?"

Billy was Carfax's general dirty-tricks agent. "Not as far as I know. I think even Julien wouldn't risk Billy among his guests."

David watched Julien bow over Nan Lucan's hand. "I'm never sure which Julien we're dealing with. St. Juste, the agent from the Continent, whom even O'Roarke is afraid of, my cousin Julien, who plays with the children with an ease I envy, or my cousin Arthur, who liked to make mischief just for the fun of it."

"Not just for the fun of it, I think. Not even then."

"No, perhaps not. I don't think I ever realized how hard it was for him."

"You were child."

"Still." David's gaze went to his cousin, who had moved on from the Lucans and was now speaking to the Duke of Wellington. "I hope he knows he's playing with fire."

"I'm quite sure he does."

"Has he met Wellington?" David asked, as though the thought had just occurred to him.

"I introduced them in Westminster a month since."

"That's not what I meant. Has he met Wellington on missions?"

"In numerous disguises, apparently."

"What are you looking so solemn about?" David's lover, Simon, joined them and leaned his arm against the wall beside David. He looked more at ease than Malcolm had ever seen him in Carfax House, probably in part because it no was longer the home of David's parents, but also because David's no longer being the heir to the title and other events the previous winter had caused Hubert Mallinson to be far more accepting of David and Simon's relationship.

"My cousin's playing with fire," David said.

Simon glanced at Julien, still conversing with Wellington. "Somehow I think St. Ju—Julien—juggles fire in his sleep."

"He's met Wellington in disguise," David said.

"He's probably met half the room in disguise," Malcolm said. "I think he has a very shrewd idea about what he's setting up tonight. What he and Kitty are setting up. They don't need to play the beau monde's game, but they know it can be useful."

"I don't think he's going to be bored as Lord Carfax," Simon said.

"No," David said. "He's made that abundantly clear. Good God." David gaped in a way he almost never did. "Is that Lady Shroppington?"

Malcolm watched Lady Shroppington, her gray hair adorned with plumes, fine diamonds sparkling round her throat and at her ears, exchange greetings with Emily Cowper. In whose box Lady Shroppington's paid assassin had concealed a rifle that they had narrowly prevented him from using six months since. "Yes, Julien wanted her here."

David clutched the stem of his champagne glass as though he was afraid he'd drop it. "I understand Sam Lucan. He's a friend. I understand Beverston, for all he's a member of the League. Because he's a member of the League. I even understand Sylvie St. Ives, because Julien wants to keep an eye on her because of their past association. But Lady Shroppington—"

"Julien's as interested in his enemies as his friends," Malcolm said. Lady Shroppington was connected—in ways they hadn't yet determined—to the faction trying to take over the Elsinore League. The faction selling the papers to Hubert Mallinson tonight.

"She tried to kill his wife." David cast a quick glance at Simon. She'd tried to have him killed too, along with Kit Montagu and their friend Mr. Hapgood. Both of whom were also present tonight.

"And Julien said he'd be more comfortable keeping an eye on her," Malcolm said.

"But the risk—"

"I doubt she'll try to attack Kitty or anyone else in the midst of the ball," Malcolm said. "If she was inclined to attempt anything, she'd be more likely to hire an assassin when she *wasn't* present. Besides, once the information about Antonio Barosa was published, Kitty and the rest of you were no longer a threat to her. The information's out in the open and it doesn't seem to have had the effect she feared."

"And we're all still wondering what we missed," Simon murmured.

"Quite." Malcolm had gone over the papers Kitty and the others had smuggled out of Spain and secretly published until he knew them by heart, searching for whatever secret they contained that Lady Shroppington and those she was working in the League were ready to kill to conceal. Last January, Lady Shroppington and the League had gone to rather extraordinary lengths to prevent the publication of notes of meetings the former Lord Carfax had had with a Spanish contact and an Italian emissary called Antonio Barossa. Malcolm hadn't been able to find any trail of the real Antonio Barossa. Which might mean the name was an alias used by an agent, as they suspected. And might support Raoul's theory that it was an alias for the man trying to take over the League, also known as Alexander Radford, though that was almost certainly not his real name either.

"She also tried to have Sir Horace Smytheton killed at the Tavistock," David pointed out. "And he's here too."

Sir Horace was dancing with his wife, the actress Jennifer Mansfield, as though he hadn't a care in the world. Jennifer, far more cautious, also appeared to be enjoying herself. Though Malcolm had no doubt her senses were finely tuned. She was a very capable former agent. "Lady Shroppington wouldn't move against Smytheton herself, and as with the others, she's less likely to try something when she's present. And more important, the League haven't tried anything against Sir Horace for almost six months." Though they still hadn't been able to discover why the League had targeted Smytheton, who had once been a League member himself.

"And we're supposed to greet her as though nothing has happened." David was still staring at Lady Shroppington.

"When all else fails, seek refuge in social niceties," Simon said. "Or in your acting ability. We were all quite proficient when we met at Oxford. Pretend we're doing *Harry IV, part 1* again. With all the political intriguing and various factions, tonight isn't that different."

"Lucan." Julien extended his hand to Sam Lucan, who had gone by the name Sancho Lugo in the days when he'd been the most reliable supplier of guns in the Iberian Peninsula, with a smile of genuine warmth. "Mrs. Lucan." He turned to Nan, red-haired and exuberant, whom Sam had had the good sense to marry. "I'm glad you could come."

Nan shook her head. "Still can't get used to the name."

"I think Kitty shares your feeling about being Lady Carfax," Julien said. "I hope your daughter is well. You must bring her to play with the children again some time."

"Thank you." Nan's smile was a bit easier, as though perhaps the reminder of playing with the children on the drawing room carpet made Carfax House a bit less intimidating. Julien could sympathize. He found it intimidating himself, and the children's toys scattered about on a normal day did a great deal to humanize it. Odd to have them tidied away now.

Sam was regarding Julien as though he were a tiger with a jeweled collar. "Good of you to invite us, St. Ju—Carfax."

"Good of you to come," Julien said. "I can well understand it seems something of a risk."

"Blimey," Nan said.

"Your husband is understandably somewhat wary of me, Mrs. Lucan. But you of all people must understand the advantage of a reputation. I was never nearly as lethal as I let on."

Sam nearly spluttered over his champagne. "Don't believe that for a moment."

Julien clapped him on the shoulder. "It's good to have friends here."

"Is that what we are?" Sam started to wipe his mouth, then appeared to remember he was wearing gloves.

"I'm learning to have friends. It's a novelty I quite enjoy."

4

"*R*annoch."

"Sandy." Malcolm turned from scanning the crowd to smile at Sandy Trenor. "I was hoping to see you. At the risk of a cliché, it really is a crush."

"It's a splendid party." Sandy grinned with youthful enthusiasm. "You have no idea how many people envied our being invited. The Carfaxes are the talk of London."

"Not surprising, given everything."

"No, but it's more than that. You can tell just looking at them. You could tell from St. Jus—devil take it, I can't manage to call him Carfax—Julien's speech in the Lords. If not before."

"Yes. I think you're right. Kitty and Julien are making it very clear what sort of presence they mean to have in London. And how much things have changed."

"It was good of them to invite us. And Lucan and Nan." Sandy and Sam Lucan could not be more different, but Sandy's mistress, Bet Simcox, was Nan Lucan's sister.

Sandy cast a glance about and took a step closer to Malcolm. "See here, Rannoch, can you help look after Bet tonight? We have a lot of friends here, but there are far more people she doesn't know, and you know how overwhelming it can be. My parents are here, and I'm going to have to speak with them at some point."

"And you don't want a scene."

Sandy grimaced but didn't look away. "I don't want Bet made uncomfortable. And yes, I don't want a scene if we can help it. Mama's likely to try to get me to dance with eligible girls, even with Bet here. It's got worse lately." He frowned. "Perhaps I shouldn't have insisted Bet come."

"I can see the challenge for both of you. But I don't think hiding is the solution. I imagine it means quite a bit to Bet that you want her to be present." Malcolm nearly found himself asking Sandy what his intentions were when it came to Bet. But it wasn't his place to do so, of course. And he couldn't pretend it would be easy for the couple. Lewis Thornsby had been killed on the orders of his own great-aunt, Lady Shroppington, largely because he'd wanted to marry an actress. Which many would consider a more eligible match than a former prostitute.

Malcolm touched Sandy on the shoulder. "We're very fond of Bet."

Sandy gave a quick smile, the sort that put Malcolm in mind of his son Colin. While at the same time at the back of Sandy's eyes there was a knowledge that hadn't been there even a year and a half ago. "You're very kind to both of us. When we're with you and your friends, I forget sometimes—" Sandy looked down into his drink and shifted his weight from one foot to the other. "I'm not really comfortable anymore the places we can't go together. I don't enjoy it. And that includes visits to my parents."

So easy to say his parents would come round. But if they did so, they'd be a rare exception in the beau monde rather than the rule. And though Sandy and Bet lived quietly, her past was too well known for Malcolm to invent a fictional history for her, as he once had for his agent Rachel Garnier, who had worked in a brothel in Brussels.

"It's challenging," Malcolm said. "Having to be a different person with different people. Even without the complication of being agents, we wear a lot of masks in life."

Sandy gave a quick nod. "But—one can't live one's life in different pieces forever, can one?"

"People do." Gentleman often effectively had entire second families with their mistresses. The regent, now the king, had kept his marriage to Mrs. Fitzherbert going after he married Princess Caroline, as well as having numerous other mistresses, though whether his marriage to Caroline had ever been real enough to be called a life was certainly open to question. "Julien used to live his life in more pieces than I could count."

"Yes, but even he didn't want to do that forever."

Sandy had a way of coming up with unexpected wisdom. "Very true," Malcolm said.

Sandy nodded and took a drink of champagne, as though contemplating his future.

"Trenor. We've been looking for you." Kit Montagu clapped a hand on Sandy's shoulder. "Sorry, Malcolm, you too, but we need Trenor and Bet to make up a set." Kit, a committed member of the Levellers, a group of young Radicals centered round the Tavistock Theatre, was usually focused and serious, but now he was grinning, gaze alight.

"Er—of course," Sandy said. "Who else is in the set?"

"Sofia and I and Nerezza and Ben."

Sofia, Kit's bride of two months, slipped through the crowd with her friend Nerezza Russo and Nerezza's beau, Benedict Smythe.

"Sorry, Malcolm," Sofia said. "You and Mélanie could be in the set instead, but we assumed you'd be engaged."

"Mélanie is and I should be," Malcolm said. "But you're the soul of tact, Sofia."

"Where's Bet?" Nerezza asked Sandy.

"With Nan." Sandy glanced round the room. Malcolm

wondered if he was looking for Bet or his parents or both. Kit, Sofia, and Benedict were part of Sandy's world, but Nerezza was an outsider like Bet. Sandy looked back at the others and grinned. "We'd love to make up part of the set."

"Then go and find her, man." Kit tightened his hand on Sandy's shoulder, then took Sofia's arm. Sofia had worked with the Carbonari in Italy and broken the Elsinore League's codes. Nerezza had worked undercover against the League in Italy and had escaped their agents with Sofia's help. Even Benedict, fresh-faced and innocent of intrigue six months ago, had acquired an edge since he'd learned his father was an Elsinore League member and Nerezza had been threatened. But for the moment, all five of them looked like young people at a ball. Which they were, even if they happened to be agents as well.

Sandy cast a quick look at Malcolm. "Find Bet and enjoy yourself," Malcolm said. "And don't worry about the older generation."

Sofia laughed, Kit gave a mock salute, the others grinned, and they went off, laughing.

JULIEN SURVEYED the ballroom as he moved through the crowd, pausing to exchange greetings, to offer a compliment, to perform an introduction. Keeping an eye out for George Dalton. And offering plentiful distraction so the others could devote more serious energies to the attempt to thwart Dalton in selling the papers. It was easy enough to be a distraction tonight. It would have been more difficult not to gather atten-tion as he moved about the ballroom. His father's ballroom. His uncle's. And now his own. And yet many of the eyes turned on him regarded him as an interloper.

His   paternal   God-knows-how-many-times-removed Mallinson grandfather had crossed the Channel with the bastard of Normandy and managed to survive the Battle of Hastings and get a barony out of it. Which a Wars-of-the-Roses Mallinson did enough double-dealing to turn into a viscountcy, and an enterprising courtier with a good leg that caught Elizabeth's eye turned into an earldom. Not long after this first Earl Carfax started building Carfax Court with the merchant's daughter he married, Julien's maternal great-great-great-grandfather Daniel Fletcher had set sail for Jamaica. He was a tanner's son and traveled between decks. But he still had a far easier voyage than Julien's grandmother's ancestors, whose names Julien didn't know, who came on a slave ship a bit later. They all made their lives in an alien country, but his grandmother's people hadn't had any choice about leaving. Or about how to make their lives when they got there. Daniel Fletcher dreamt of founding a fortune in the new world and became a privateer with Sir Henry Morgan. He probably did far better for himself than he would have done toiling on the land. He ended up with a sizable property in Jamaica and married the governor's niece. He was apparently a good businessman, which Julien suspected most successful pirates were. By the time his great-grandson, also named Daniel, was born, the family had property in Barbados as well. The younger Daniel was a second son and inherited the Barbados property. He did well out of sugarcane, but he did even better trading other people's sugar to Britain and the Continent. He had a tidy fortune and he wasn't bad looking, judging by the portraits, so he must have had a number of match-making mamas scheming and their daughters setting their caps at him.

Julien cast a glance round the ballroom where much of the same activity was underway. It wasn't particularly surprising Daniel had taken a liking to one of his slaves or even that he made Julia his mistress and installed her in his house. What was surprising was that instead of marrying one of the local girls, Daniel took Julia with him on one of his trips to Britain to negotiate trading contacts and freed her and married her. It would have been legal for him to marry her in Barbados, but it would have been more of a scandal, to say the least. It was enough of a scandal as it was, though somewhat lessened by the fact that she died giving birth to Julien's mother, Pamela, not long after they returned.

At least she died free, someone had once said to him. Julien's fingers tightened round his champagne glass.

Kitty, of course, would say no wife is really free, legally. A wife couldn't control her own fortune unless her family were very careful with the marriage settlement, she couldn't deny her body to her husband, and her husband could deny her access to her children. Julien was still rather stunned that Kitty had agreed to marry, considering what marriage signified. But it was true his grandmother Julia hadn't been a slave when she died. Julian and her sister had come from another planation where their mother was the owner's mistress. The man who owned them and sold them was their father. Even assuming he hadn't taken their mother against her will, one couldn't possibly say their mother, Julien's great-grandmother, had acted freely. Could a person owned by another person ever give themselves freely to that person? At the very least, the person who claimed to own the other person could never be sure.

Julien looked across the ballroom and felt his fingers curl tighter round the crystal stem. He'd crossed a number of lines in his life. But he'd never slept with anyone, man or woman, who wasn't willing. That was one line he couldn't imagine crossing. He drew a breath. For a moment, his mother's description of the hibiscus-tinged air was so vivid it flooded his senses. He didn't know how his grandmother Julia had felt about his grandfather Daniel. His mother had never known her own mother. His nurse told him Julia had been grateful to Daniel, which perhaps was something. Daniel seemed to have loved Julia—or what he'd have called love. He never remarried. He took her sister as a mistress and had more children. Julien's cousin in Canada, whom he corresponded with, was a cousin through both his grandmother and his grandfather. His mother had grown up playing with half-siblings who were slaves. And an aunt who looked after her and shared her father's bed who was also a slave. Julien had never got to talk to her about that. He wondered sometimes if she'd have tried to explain when he was older, if she had lived. Daniel had seen to it she had the best education—dancing masters, music masters, drawing masters. A governess he brought from France. She couldn't mingle in society in Barbados, so when she was seventeen he took her to London and got one of his aristocratic contacts to take her about. Generous funds must have been involved, because between his commercial ties, the general bias against the West Indian planter class, and her mother's having been a slave, it wouldn't have been easy. On the other hand, it was easier in London than it would have been in Barbados. And at that point, Daniel's fortune was large enough to command a great deal of attention.

Julien wasn't sure if Daniel had been pleased with the Carfax match because he thought being a countess would make his daughter happy, or because having an earl for a son-in-law would add to his consequence, or if he persuaded himself of the first because of the second, but he evidently considered it a great coup. He'd come back from Barbados for Julien's christening, but he died not long after, so Julien had no memory of him. Daniel hadn't freed his slaves when he died. Julien's father, John Mallinson, had inherited the plantation and the trading business, which also meant he owned Julien's aunts and uncles and cousins. He engaged one of Daniel's nephews to continue to run the planation. The nephew and his family had died in the *Unicorn* Rebellion that Julien had helped arm. The house burned in the rebellion but was rebuilt. Julien's Uncle Hubert, who had been Lord Carfax for twenty-five years, had never visited, but hired someone to run the plantation. He had owned Julien's cousins. If Julien hadn't—disappeared—he could have freed them decades sooner.

As he recalled the past, Julien moved among his guests. Stopping to accept the good wishes of friends of his father who had known him as a boy, to greet parliamentary colleagues Malcolm had introduced him to in recent weeks, to welcome the few personal friends among the throng. Not to mention smiling at a number of enemies. He could do it all with one eye peeled for George Dalton while his mind dwelled on the past of the family that had got him to this point. And then an unexpectedly apt comment cut through his recollections.

"I've heard about you, Carfax. You're the abolitionist."

Julien stared at the man before him. Lord Wharton. A Whig politician, according to Malcolm more known for the quality of the port in his cellar, funded by his wife's generous dowry, than for his political convictions. "Among other things," Julien said with an easy smile.

Wharton sneezed and snapped his snuff box shut. "Not a good way to go on, speaking on abolition when the Whigs hadn't decided it was time to bring it up."

"The Whigs didn't bring it up. I did. I don't go in for high-flown rhetoric, but I believe the party believes in individual conscience."

"Ha. Never confuse rhetoric with the reality on the ground."

"And I believe I've read certain words about being created equal and the dignity and freedom of the individual."

"Is that what you were doing all these years you were gone? Becoming a Jacobin?"

"I didn't need to leave Britain to know that the color of a person's skin shouldn't render him or her subservient to another. "

Wharton frowned at Julien as though examining something under a microscope. "You're an intellectual."

"Hardly. But I did read John Locke one summer when I was bored. Also Paine. Also Cugoano, who should certainly understand slavery, having been a slave."

"We all—well, the Whigs and a lot of the Tories—agree slavery's a bad thing. It's the timing of getting rid of it."

"It seemed timely to me. I'd just affirmed the freedom of the slaves on the Carfax estates in Barbados. Which was long overdue."

"You mean you freed your slaves."

"They were never legitimately enslaved. But yes, I made it clear their freedom was legally affirmed."

"You'll never get an income from the estates now."

"You'll have to ask the former slaves about that. I turned the estates over to them."

Wharton spluttered champagne over his cravat. "You did what?"

"If anyone knows how to manage the estates, they do. And it keeps the estates in the family. After all, a number of the former slaves are my cousins."

"You're a fool, Carfax."

Odd how the name still hit him like a blast of scalding water. "Quite possibly."

"You'll lose your investment."

"I already have. As I said, I signed it over to the people who had been working it. So it's not my concern anymore, strictly speaking. But for their sakes, I hope they can make a go of it."

"They'll be run out of Barbados."

"I don't think so. Not with the extra funding I've provided. One thing I've learned in my time in numerous parts of the globe is that money has a way of talking."

"Is this how you're thinking of making a name for yourself?"

"By helping former slaves achieve freedom? There are far worse things to be known for."

"Abolition." Wharton drew out the word. "If you make it

your topic when the party's not ready, you won't get far. Even Radicals need to learn to play the game. Look at Brougham."

"Difficult not to look at him just now." Julien glanced across the ballroom at Henry Brougham, who was waltzing with Cordelia. "He has a way of putting himself center stage. We certainly agree on a number of a number of issues. Very much including abolition. And believe me, I know rather a bit about how to play any number of games."

"Have you given thought to what you're unleashing? There's no denying slaves are capable of great violence. Even Wilberforce tempered his approach after Bussa's rebellion. Look at the number who died."

Bussa's rebellion had come some twenty years after the *Unicorn* rebellion Julien had helped arm. The results had arguably been far more tragic. But then, the aim of the *Unicorn* rebels had been to escape Barbados, which they had managed to accomplish. Far easier, perhaps, than taking control of the whole island. "Surely that would only reinforce the idea that if they were free, they'd have no need to rebel to gain their freedom."

"You're placing a lot of faith in reason. That sort isn't rational."

"What sort would that be?" Julien inquired. "You must forgive me, I may not be rational enough to understand."

"I had no wish to imply—of course, your own case is quite different."

"I don't see how. Plenty of slaves have three-quarters or seven-eighths European blood. If my grandfather had made my grandmother his concubine and not freed her, my mother would have been born a slave, and if my father had gone to Barbados and made her his mistress, I'd be a slave myself."

"But you're not—"

"Violent? Many would disagree with you. Even now, I could be quite violent in pursuit of my freedom and the freedom of my family. Or are you saying the difference is that I'm educated? In which case, the solution would seem to be to send every slave to Harrow and Oxford. Not that I got to Oxford, I left the country first."

"You're very amusing, Carfax."

"Believe me," Julien said, for once with perfect truth, "I don't find it amusing at all."

5

Nan Lucan sank down on a settee in a columned embrasure, gripping her champagne glass as though it held a precious elixir. "Didn't show too much ankle, did I?" she asked, smoothing her blue sarcenet skirt. "Funny to worry about showing too much ankle. In the old days in St. Giles we could buy our supper by showing as much as we could."

"Don't worry." Bet Simcox sat beside her sister. "A lot of the ladies here have made flashing a bit of ankle into an art. Why else do you think they embroider such pretty clocks on silk stockings?"

Nan choked on her champagne. "I don't know how you do it, Betty."

Bet twisted her fan on its silk string round her wrist and let her shawl slither about her. "I don't that much, not really. I mean, I'm not invited a lot of places Sandy is." She cast a glance round the ballroom. It had grown more crowded just in the short time it had taken her and Nan to make a half circuit round the edge. "His parents are supposed to be here tonight. I don't want them to cut me in front of him and embarrass him."

Nan frowned. She had always had dramatic brows, and she'd plucked them with extra care for tonight, into an arch many of the great ladies present would envy. "You're a proper lady now."

"Not really." Bet smoothed a fold of her lace overdress. Mélanie Rannoch had taken her to order the gown, ivory lace over blush-colored satin, from her modiste, Marthe. "I've just learned to talk differently. It doesn't change who I am on the inside."

"Oh, well." Nan took a drink of champagne. "Nothing does that. Not even for people like Mr. St. Juste. He's still the same even though he's Lord Carfax."

"Funny. I hadn't thought of it that way." Mostly what she'd thought was how happy Kitty and Julien were and what marriage obviously meant to them both, though they wouldn't admit it. "But I think it has been difficult for them. I don't know that they'd have chosen this life. Still, they were born to it, so that makes a difference. No one questions that they belong."

"I'm not so sure about that. She's Spanish. Sam would tell you people don't forget that, fine lady or no. And his mother wasn't one of them either." Nan looked at the crowd swirling before them in a blur of airy skirts, glossy ringlets, flashing jewels, sweeping coattails, and gleaming cravats. "Seems like there are a lot of outsiders here, one way and another."

"Yes, that's true. Perhaps it's what makes Mr. St. Ju—Lord Carf—Julien sympathetic to us." Bet frowned, because it was odd to think of Julien's being unsure about anything. And certainly, circling the room now, he seemed supremely confi-dent, as Kitty had when she'd greeted them at the head of the stairs. Yet she'd seen them enough to recognize their acting skills. "I do hope tonight goes well."

Nan cast a sidelong glance at her. "You're worried about Sam and me causing trouble."

"No!" Bet gripped her sister's hand, tightly because she couldn't bear to say that Nan's words were closer to the mark than she'd admit. "I'm glad you're here. Truly. I just don't like to make things awkward for Sandy. It's an odd world."

"You're more comfortable in that world than you realize, Bet."

Bet pulled her shawl about her shoulders. It was a pink-flowered silk Sandy had given her shortly after she moved into his rooms. From Italy. Funny, the beau monde prized things from faraway places, but they tended to look askance at people who hadn't come from within their midst for generations. Whether that meant being born in Spain, or Barbados, or St. Giles. Which probably seemed even further away than the first two to most of those present tonight. She didn't feel comfortable in this world. Sandy's world. And yet—she no longer wondered which fork or knife to use with which course. She understood the order of introductions, when to take off her bonnet and gloves. She could receive callers and pour tea. She knew the steps of fashionable dances and not to dance more than twice with the same gentleman. She'd learned a smattering of French and a bit of Italian. When she was included in invitations, she knew how to respond to them, and how to pen a thank-you note. Sometimes she was so focused on all the ways she didn't belong that she lost sight of how much had changed.

"I'll always be an outsider. As long as—" As long as her relationship with Sandy lasted. She had been living in Sandy's flat for a year and a half and she still couldn't answer how long the arrangement would last. It wasn't unusual for a young man in Sandy's situation to keep a mistress. It was unusual for them to share the same lodgings. She had moved in with Sandy because she'd been in danger and Sandy had insisted on protecting her. She had stayed because his brother had been sent off in disgrace and Sandy had needed her. Almost eighteen months later she was still there. But somehow, at some point, something was going to change.

Nan sent her a shrewd look. "He loves you, Betty. And it's not just calf love."

Bet clasped her hands together, gripping the opal ring Sandy had given her beneath her glove. "You know it's not about love, Nan."

"Well, not just about love, maybe. But that's part of it. How often did I swear I'd never get married?"

"That's different. You and Sam are the same."

"Ha. We're like oil and water sometimes."

"You're the same in the ways that matter."

"What are the ways that matter?"

Bet pleated a fold of her skirt between her fingers. The lace felt rough through her gloves. "The people who love you aren't trying to pull you apart."

"I don't think the people who really love you and Sandy would do that either."

"His parents love him. I've never properly met them, but I've heard enough to know that."

"The regent—the king—married a princess. Can't get much more suitable than that, and look how it turned out. Seems like trying to push them to make a proper marriage had all sorts of bad effects."

"Lord Carfax." Sylvie St. Ives's voice stopped Julien as he crossed the ballroom. There was only one reason Sylvie would have been found unengaged in a ballroom since she'd turned sixteen. Because she wanted private conversation. And not just to catch up with an old friend. Assuming the term even applied to them. Of all the people in the ballroom who might want the papers Uncle Hubert was buying from George Dalton, Sylvie was certainly high on the list.

"Lady St. Ives," Julien said. "Thank you for coming."

Sylvie opened her eyes very wide. They were the same clear, deep blue they had been when Julien first met her in childhood. That blue gaze had been every bit as deceptive then as now. "You can't have thought I'd miss it. I suppose I should thank you for inviting me. But then, I expect you wanted to see how I would behave."

"Yes," Julien said. "I did."

Sylvie tilted her head to one side. "I never thought I'd see you come to this. Even when you were lolling on a picnic blanket with the children and looking at Kitty Ashford with a sickeningly sweet expression."

"I'm glad I can still surprise you."

She smoothed her fan as though it were a knife. The sticks were polished steel. Knowing Sylvie, he wouldn't be surprised if one was a stiletto. He'd once had a similar fan he'd used when masquerading as a woman. "I should have known you'd want it back," she said. "Difficult to give up power. And difficult to escape Carfax's control."

"Aren't those two in contradiction?"

Sylvie unfurled the fan. "Tell me you aren't doing precisely what Carfax wants right now."

It was, Julien had to admit, a fair point. One that occasionally troubled him. "Let's say our interests have aligned in some things. For the moment."

"Fascinating how he always manages to win."

Beneath her light, brittle voice was the bitterness of the teenager who had been Hubert Mallinson's creature. In part because she'd helped Julien. "Sylvie—" A debt he'd never be able to repay, no matter what he thought of Sylvie now, hung between them. "I haven't come close to forgiving him."

"But you've made peace with him."

"Let's say we've reached a truce. For now."

"You're fond of him."

The moment he and Uncle Hubert had agreed to Julien's

taking over the title flashed into Julien's mind. "My feelings for Uncle Hubert have always been—complicated."

Sylvie wielded her fan, gesturing about the ballroom where his friends and enemies swirled on the dance floor and sipped champagne. Somehow the languid motion was as if she'd held a dagger point to his throat. "Do you think this will make you happy?"

"What? Being Carfax? Living here? Hosting a ball? Being married to Kitty and a father? Yes to the last. For the others—I think I can be happy with them, which is a bit different."

She shook her head. "You never used to even talk about happiness."

He dug his shoulder into the cold marble of a column. "I know."

She snapped the fan closed. "I told you it would bore you, with time. I still think it will."

"I don't think so. But we won't know until time passes."

Sylvie's gaze locked on his own, less antagonist now than friend trying to get a point across. "It's not that one falls out of love. It's that love isn't enough."

"For whom? The lover or the beloved?"

"Both."

"I can't answer for Kitty. I wouldn't burden her with expecting her to find me enough to build her life on. And I don't expect to build my life round her. That would be a burden as well. The jury's still out on what sort of husband I'll make, but I'd have made a damnable one until lately, when I learned to live with myself. But I also know I don't want to live without her. And I flatter myself she doesn't want to live without me."

Sylvie regarded him for a moment, head tilted to the side, the blonde ringlets he'd often threaded through his fingers falling against her cheek. "Even knowing you as well as I do, I can't decide."

"What?"

"If you really are besotted or if this is an elaborate pose. I can read the way you look at her. I've never seen you look at a woman that way before. But you're good enough to be able to counterfeit that for the right reason."

"What would that be?" Julien inquired.

"I don't know. To make us all complacent, perhaps." She watched him for a moment, like a commander scouting familiar terrain where the enemy may be lying concealed. "You're a creature of the jungle, Julien. As I am. Even more than your marriage, what I can't make out is what you were doing with your speech in Parliament."

"Really? I thought it was fairly coherent."

"Oh, it was, on the surface. But I haven't the least idea what you were trying to accomplish."

"I'll admit emancipation still seems in the future, but you know I relish a challenge."

"Julien, for heaven's sake, the one thing you were always free of was sentimentality. It's not as though you helped the *Unicorn* rebels to strike a blow for freedom."

Julien's actions in the *Unicorn* rebellion had sent him into exile for a quarter century. "Didn't I?"

Sylvie regarded him over the edge of her fan as though he'd suddenly transformed into a satyr. "Next you'll be joining the Sons of Africa."

"It's not a bad idea. If they'd have me."

She lifted her brows. "You've hardly been fighting for freedom for anyone all these years. And now you want to expend all your energy on black slaves?"

"We pick our fights. This one strikes me as rather important."

Her gaze shot over his face. "It mattered to you, didn't it? All those years ago. I thought you were just striking a blow at your father. But you thought you were striking one for freedom too."

He felt the bones of his shoulder boring into the Carrara marble of the column. "Is that so surprising?"

"It is of the man I thought you were."

He smiled and felt the tang of regret as much as the sting of bitterness. "It would hardly be the first time either of us was mistaken in the other."

~

"Carfax speaks well." The Hon. William Barrington, Whig MP, took a drink of port. "The new Carfax, that is. More of a flair for it than his uncle."

"Yes, he has a way with words," Malcolm agreed.

"So he does. Also quite a style of delivery." Barrington regarded Malcolm. "Thought I detected something of your tone in his abolition speech."

"I may have reviewed a draft. So may Mélanie. But the crafting of the speech was his."

"It attracted notice. Which I suspect was his intention."

"I wouldn't doubt it. But nor would I doubt that he believes passionately in his subject." Odd words to use about the former Julien St. Juste. But Malcolm had no doubt they were true.

"It was a bold move, if perhaps not the wisest one." Barrington frowned. He wasn't known for his own speeches but for his efforts rounding up votes behind the scenes. "Everyone's asking how he's going to position himself. Is abolition his issue?"

"I think he's interested in justice. In a number of ways."

"He could be a good asset. Can we count on him?"

"For what? You can count on him to stand up for what he believes in."

"Humph." Barrington took a swig of port. "That's the trouble with fellows who have no need of office or support from the party. They're too damn likely to strike out on their own. Or perhaps I should have said you're too damned likely. You don't need us either, Rannoch."

"The new Lord Carfax's sympathies certainly lie with the Whigs."

"Ha. Never thought I'd hear the words 'Whig' and 'Carfax' coupled. But are you sure you don't mean with the Radicals?"

"Very likely."

"Like your own sympathies."

"He's his own man. But you can count on both of us for most votes."

"And in the matter of the queen?" Henry Brougham, who among other things was the queen's advocate, strolled up to join them.

"I believe the queen has been ill used," Malcolm said. "So does Julien. Carfax."

"The queen could be the key to advancing our agenda," Brougham said.

"The queen is a woman who has been in an appalling situation since she married our present king."

"And she's a public figure," Barrington said. "Like queens before her. My God, Rannoch. I know you don't need office for the financial benefits, but surely you appreciate what we could do if we were in power. Electoral reform. Catholic Emancipation. Abolition when the time is right."

"When the time is right."

"Which will be never if the Tories remain in power." Barrington regarded Malcolm. "Which I know has been for all of your adult lifetime. Trust me, things could be different."

"I believe that," Malcolm said. "The question is how different?"

"Given what we have now, does that really matter?" Brougham asked.

"Yes. When one weighs the degree of compromise that's worth it."

Barrington grinned. "You're starting to think like a politician, Rannoch."

"I'm not sure if that's a compliment or an insult."

"Nor am I, truth to tell." Barrington clapped Malcolm on the shoulder, nodded at Brougham, and moved on to speak to Lord Grey.

Brougham watched Malcolm a moment. "You know how strongly I believe in abolition. You know even the slightest advantage could tip the scales for the queen and against the king. And in doing so, sever the king from his Tory cronies."

"I'm not entirely convinced the last would happen. But I take your point."

"So I may depend upon you to do anything in your power to help?"

"What do you have in mind, Brougham?" Malcolm asked.

"I have it on good authority that there are letters that could support the queen's case."

Malcolm took a drink of champagne, as casually as possible. "Surely, letters—"

"Anything could tip the balance. Carfax—Hubert Mallinson —is trying to buy them." Brougham's gaze settled on Malcolm's face. "But I expect you already know that."

"What makes you think that?"

"Don't underrate yourself, Rannoch. I certainly don't do that."

"Don't overrate me, Henry."

"I'd never do that either." Brougham took a drink of champagne himself, holding Malcolm with his gaze the entire time. "So I assume if you have the papers, you'll know what to do with them."

"My dear Henry. You're far too shrewd to assume anything."

6

"*Lord* Carfax." A woman's voice assailed Julien as he led Laura off the dance floor. Lady Harley, who had been a friend of his father's. Very likely a mistress. Her hair was the same gold it had been a quarter century ago. But then, Julien himself knew all about the uses of hair dye.

"Or perhaps I should say Arthur." Lady Harley tapped him on the arm with her fan. "After all, I've known you since you were a boy. Your father would be glad to see you back here."

"I sincerely doubt that, ma'am."

"Don't be naughty, Arthur. He'd rather you had it than his brother." She glanced up at the stuccoed ceiling Julien's father had commissioned when he redid the house. "After all, he built all this."

"So he did. And you probably have more insights than I do into what he'd have wanted to become of it. But then, I can scarcely claim to have known my father. If you'll excuse us, Lady Harley."

"Nothing like old family friends who think they know one," Laura said as they moved towards the French windows.

"She didn't really know me at all. Though I think she knew

my father quite intimately. When he first married my mother. In the days when he was redoing the house." Julien looked at the plaster ceiling again and then at the gilding on the French windows that had also been part of the renovation when his father added the balcony. "My mother's fortune turned Carfax House into what it is. Which means it was built on the back of slaves. Including a number of my mother's relatives. My relatives."

Laura watched him for a moment. Julien felt himself flush. It was not a way he usually talked. At least, not so bluntly. Laura had a quality of listening that made people confide.

"Gold," she said. "It's the lure in the New World with its so-called Indians. And also the lure in India itself. We do it a bit differently there. But there's still a denial of humanity."

Julien met her gaze and nodded.

"I grew up in it," Laura said. In figured bronze silk, pearls round her throat and at her ears and in her titian hair, she was the picture of a Mayfair lady. But something in her gaze cut through to the hard reality beneath the façade of life in the beau monde. "I can't say I didn't know what the British were doing was wrong, because a part of me understood it was, even when I was far too young to articulate it. I spoke up at times. Partly because I believed it was wrong, partly to shock people."

Past scenes, many in this house, shot through Julien's mind. "I know a bit about that."

"But I can't claim to have fought it. We deny the humanity of people who happen to look a bit different. Of course, my husband would point out we do the same for the Irish, who look like us. All it takes is an excuse to draw some sort of artificial boundary. And British fortunes are built on the backs of those very people we claim couldn't be British."

"Such as the fortune I've just inherited."

"And the one settled on me by my first husband's family.

They had holdings in India. My late father-in-law was almost the definition of unscrupulous."

"My father could have given him a run for his money. They may well have been colleagues." Laura's first husband's father, the Duke of Trenchard, had been a prominent member of the Elsinore League. Questions about his own father that he wasn't quite ready to confront shot into Julien's mind like bits of broken glass poking through the cloth one tried to use to tidy them away.

Laura met his gaze with the look of one who felt those same cuts. "So they may."

"So you've started a school with your inheritance."

"It puts some of the money to use. There's so much injustice in the world one can almost begin anywhere and feel one's making a difference."

"A polite way of telling me I've done far too little."

"On the contrary. I heard your speech. More than that, I've seen other things you've done. My husband's been fighting his whole life, and I know he often wonders what it's for."

"Yes, I've called O'Roarke some unpleasant things. Which rather justified my own lack of action."

"Seeming lack."

"You're too kind, Laura."

"Or perhaps perceptive. Agonizing over past actions is singularly useless, as my husband would say. But he wonders more often than I'd like if he's simply been beating his head against a wall."

"Your husband inspired and continues to inspire a number of people. Including me. Though I'm damned if I'll ever let him see it."

"I rather think he does."

Julien found himself grinning. "O'Roarke is far too acute."

Laura smiled in response. "I tell him sometimes that if he could just see how it matters to his children, he'd realize how much it was worth it. They'll remember what he's done when they look back at this time. As will others, I trust. But even they should give him hope."

Julien felt a mantle settle over him that was still not familiar. "It changes one, being a parent. I remember the day I learned about Genny. The world had a clarity I'd never known before. At the same time, I felt as though if I put one foot wrong, I'd smash through glass."

"I know the feeling. Though with a bit of time, one learns to just muddle through."

"The wonder never quite goes away, though. At least, it hasn't for me." For a moment he saw the children upstairs in the nursery, when he'd smuggled ices up half an hour since. "I don't think I'd want it to. Terrifying as the responsibility is."

"No," Laura agreed. "It hits one all over again at unexpected moments."

Julien looked across the room. "I'll never really know what it was like for my mother. Growing up as she did. Viewed as an outsider. With cousins who were her father's property. And I'll certainly never understand what it was like for those cousins. Or for my grandmother, or my great-grandmother, who died a slave. I don't suppose my mother could fully understand their lives either. Whatever else she endured, she grew up in luxury. I'm not sure I ever want Genny to understand it. But I think it's desperately important that she does, as much as she can. And the boys."

Laura nodded. "I think it's one of the greatest challenges for a teacher. Or a parent. Helping children see how the world looks through someone else's eyes."

Julien looked across the room. "There's a lot of injustice in the world. One finds it back to Homer. Kitty and Mélanie would remind us that women have been treated unjustly throughout history. Davenport could give a slew of classical examples. It's all intolerable. But this is—it goes back less than three hundred years. Ancestors within our memory made this travesty. And people have been pointing out how wrong it is from the start. When I really stop and think, I shudder at the injustice. And by the time I was sixteen, I thought nothing could shake me."

EMILY COWPER SMILED AT MÉLANIE. "No wonder you don't care about vouchers to Almack's. I can't tell you how many people who have no trouble being admitted to Almack's asked me with envy if I could help secure them an invitation to Carfax House tonight."

Mélanie laughed. "You know it's not like that, Em." In truth, she was quite relieved that Laura's situation as the wife of a divorced man rendered her outside the strict bounds required to be granted vouchers for Almack's and gave Mélanie an excellent excuse not to attend either. But though she had never much cared for the assemblies, and had only attended because it seemed to be part of her role as Malcolm's wife, she had grown very fond of Emily, who was one of the patronesses. In fact, for all the strictures of Almack's, most of the patronesses were quite daring and diverting, a paradox that still puzzled Mélanie.

"Some people manage to be outside society but still have society—or a good portion of it—clamor to come to them. Of course, it helps to have been born a Rannoch—or rather, the Duke of Strathdon's grandson—or a Mallinson." Emily frowned. "I can't believe it was less than a year ago I introduced Kitty Ashford—Lady Carfax—to you in my ballroom. Though I suppose it was really Malcolm who did the introducing." She unfurled her fan, peacock blue to match her gown. "I was actually concerned for you that night because Mrs. Ashford had known Malcolm in the Peninsula and it was clear they were well acquainted. I had no notion she'd known

Arthur Mallinson there as well. I had no notion Arthur Mallinson was alive." Emily looked across the ballroom at Julien, who was leaning negligently against a column and conversing with Henry Brougham and Lady Frances, Malcolm's aunt, the picture of an accomplished host. "When I look for cues, knowing who he is, I can see it. But I don't think I'd ever have recognized him. Even if I'd sat at table next to him or danced a waltz with him. Which, come to think of it, I did."

"One sees what one expects. Part of the secret of being undercover."

Emily shook her head, her glossy dark side curls stirring about her face. "But I knew Arthur. I danced with him at children's balls. My brothers played with him. I even imagined marrying him and being Countess Carfax. Which is rather an interesting thought." She glanced round the ballroom. "He was always intriguing, but I never guessed how much. Still, I can't believe I didn't know him when he appeared in London all these years later."

"You weren't looking for him. And people change a lot from fifteen to forty."

"Boys, especially. They either get even duller or much more interesting." Emily's gaze moved to Kitty, who had abandoned her post at the head of the stairs and was talking to the Duke of Wellington, smiling up at him with just the right degree of dignity, flirtation, and the sangfroid of a beau monde hostess. Julien turned his head at that precise moment and looked at Kitty. "It's probably a good thing I never let myself be too infatuated with Arthur Mallinson. He's obviously besotted with his wife." She cast a quick look at Mélanie. "Have I said something funny?"

Mélanie was looking at Julien, who had caught Kitty's gaze. Kitty echoed his smile for a moment. As in a well-crafted play, a moment could say a great deal. "Just that I'd once have laughed at the idea of Julien's being besotted with anyone. But, yes, I think he is."

"And she seems equally fond of him, for all neither of them makes a show of it. A very good thing. I thought Harry—my Harry"—Emily glanced at Lord Palmerston, who was leading Manon Harleton onto the dance floor—"was a bit too fond of her. Not, of course, that marriage necessarily changes these things, but I rather think that in their case it will."

"Yes, I think so," Mélanie said.

"She looks very comfortable," Emily said, as Kitty turned back to Wellington. "It can't be easy taking over Carfax House."

"She's a very accomplished woman. And she's good at playing a role."

"That should serve her well in London society." Emily regarded Mélanie, amusement and curiosity dancing in her gaze. "You're not going to tell me what really happened, are you?"

"Em—"

"No. I know, you can't." Emily waved her fan. "I should be used to it by now." She looked at Julien again. "He was always different. I don't mean his mother. She was beautiful and quite fascinating. But Arthur always seemed to be laughing at the world. And I always had the sense he was ten times cleverer than the rest of us. I think he'll be quite an asset to the Whigs."

"He's his own person."

"So's Malcolm. So's Mr. Brougham, for that matter, and I can't deny he's useful." She glanced at Queen Caroline's defense lawyer, now talking with Rupert Caruthers. "Much as he annoys me."

Henry Brougham had run off to the Continent three years ago with Emily's sister-in-law Caroline. Not William Lamb's wife Caro, who had been Byron's mistress, but "Caro George," who was married to George Lamb. Emily had gone to the Continent to persuade her sister-in-law home.

"Caro and George seem happy these days," Mélanie said.

Emily wrinkled her nose. "They're settled. I'm not sure it's the same thing. And, of course, there's going to be no avoiding Brougham for the next months. And he's going to take full advantage of it. Everyone's going to be taking advantage of everything they can in politics as this business between the king and queen plays out, I suspect. It's ghastly and quite fascinating. No quiet autumn in the country this year." Emily's delicate brows drew together. "One can't deny the queen has made a spectacle of herself. But she's been appallingly treated. Do you know she says she did commit adultery once but it was with the husband of Mrs. Fitzherbert?"

Maria Fitzherbert was the prince regent, now the king's, first wife, whom he had married without royal permission. The marriage was considered invalid because of the lack of royal permission. "Well said," Mélanie said.

"Yes, I thought so." Emily scanned the ballroom. "It's an eclectic crowd."

"Jul—the new Lord Carfax has a wide acquaintance."

"He's been abroad."

"A number of the people here are people he met abroad." That was true, actually. Julien had insisted on inviting people like Sam and Nan alongside his uncle and aunt and senior politicians and diplomats. "They can decide if they want to come," he'd said. And, of course, everyone was so curious they had come.

"They're going to be bohemian too, aren't they?" Emily said. "And not worry about what anyone thinks, and because they're Mallinsons they'll still be at the center of things, like you and Malcolm."

"We aren't at the center of things."

"Ha. You may manage to remove yourselves a bit because you don't go out as much, but you still receive just as much notice when you do. Possibly more. There's nothing like being sought after. And it helps your plays. And Malcolm's career." Her gaze went from Julien to Kitty. "It will be interesting to see what the Carfaxes do."

"Yes," Mélanie said. "It certainly will." She watched the crowd shift, and suddenly found herself looking at the sleek dark hair and florid profile of Sir George Dalton. She met Kitty's gaze across the room, and then Laura's, and Cordy's. It was time to go to work.

7

Cordelia, having caught Mélanie's eye, excused herself to the Duke and Duchess of Trenchard and slipped across the room towards Mélanie. Mélanie had made a similar excuse to move away from Emily Cowper. She and Cordelia met in an embrasure that had a good view of the ballroom. Which gave them an excellent view as Kitty paused to speak with a footman coming through the archway from the supper room with a tray of champagne. The picture of a conscientious hostess, a little nervous about her first ball. She couldn't have done it better, Cordelia thought. The footman moved on. Addison was a little shorter than most of the footmen engaged for the ball, but he moved with such assurance it was scarcely noticeable. He drew up beside a group that included Sir George Dalton, the tray angled just so.

Everyone took a champagne glass. Including Dalton.

"Addison's quite brilliant," Cordelia murmured to Mélanie.

"Yes, it's good to see him in action," Mélanie said, gaze on Sir George.

"Sir George." Lady Frances Davenport, Malcolm's aunt and the wife of Harry's uncle Archie, stopped beside him, her voice carrying clearly to where Cordelia stood with Mélanie. "You must advise me. Everyone says your opinion of horseflesh is unparalleled."

"Harry briefed Frances as well as Archie," Cordelia told Mélanie. "Fanny's in her element."

"I don't wonder at it. We've all been longing for action."

Frances wasn't a trained agent any more than Cordelia was, but they had both learned to love the game their husbands played.

"There's a cream-colored pair at Tattersall's I quite have my heart set on," Frances continued to Sir George in the same carrying voice, "but Archie says they're more showy than sound. I got him to agree that if you thought them reasonable, he would accede to your judgment."

"What?" Sir George blinked, not the first man to be bowled over by Lady Frances. Or the last. "Oh, glad to offer my opinion. But I'd have to see them."

"Yes, of course. I can't go with you—such a nuisance that ladies aren't allowed at Tatts—but Archie can. Only, mind you, hold firm and give your opinion, no matter what he says. He does hate to admit he's wrong."

"My cue," Cordelia whispered to Mélanie. "Aunt Frances." She swept up to the small group, drawing Mélanie with her. "Do stop monopolizing Sir George. He's promised to me for the next waltz."

"What?" Sir George's already florid face turned a bit more flushed.

"Oh, do pray play along," Cordelia said, in a lowered voice worthy of the stage. "Bobby Eustace asked me to dance, and I had to give him some excuse. The last time I waltzed with him, he trod on my flounce in three places, and my maid still hasn't been able to repair the lace properly. Surely you won't be so ungallant as to refuse?"

Cordelia smiled up at Dalton, wondering if she was laying it on a bit thick. But Sir George drew a breath and smiled down at her. "Certainly, Lady Cordelia. Anything to oblige." He extended his arm.

Cordelia circled her gloved fingers round his proffered arm and let him lead her onto the dance floor. He lurched a little as they took their places, but she couldn't be sure if that was owed to what Kitty had slipped into the glass Addison had given him or to the number of glasses he'd consumed before. She smiled at him and gathered up the folds of her gown as the first notes of the waltz sounded. He stumbled again in the opening promenade, muttered an apology, and moved with creditable grace through the first figures. Then he stumbled a third time and nearly fell.

Cordelia made to trip herself. "Oh, dear, how silly of me. Too many glasses of champagne, I fear. Do let's find somewhere to sit down."

He gave a sigh that might have been relief or a gasp for air, and let her draw him into an antechamber.

"Much better." Cordelia sank into a chair and fanned herself. "Do sit down, Sir George. You look quite red."

And he did. Though not precisely sleepy yet. Cordelia wondered just what she was going to have to do to keep him where he needed to be until the drug took effect. An attempt at flirtation would probably rouse his suspicions. There were disadvantages to having her happy marriage so generally known.

"Don't mind if I do." Sir George sank into a chair and tugged at his collar.

"Do tell me about your horses," Cordelia said, though, as he began to talk, she wondered if she'd be the one to fall asleep.

But a few minutes later, he slumped back in his chair and began to snore.

She eased the door open a few inches, then pulled it shut, her signal to Mélanie and Laura. They slipped into the room a few moments later, laughing like two friends enjoying a gossip, then went serious as soon as they closed the door.

"Like clockwork," Cordelia said. "Well, almost." She bent over Sir George. His eyes were closed, his breathing deep and rasping, but there was a difference between sleep and lack of consciousness. "How do we make sure he's out?"

Mélanie crossed to the chair and pinched Sir George's arm. He didn't stir. "Out cold." She unbuttoned his coat, tightly fitted and padded at the shoulders, and pushed it back, quickly searching for pockets. "Snuff box, watch. Here." She drew out a packet of papers tied with blue ribbon.

Cordelia let out a sigh of relief. So did Laura, almost simultaneously.

Mélanie frowned as she opened one of the papers.

"What?" Laura said. "Good God."

Cordelia moved to stand beside her friends. The paper was blank. So were all the others as Mélanie flipped through them.

"Was he planning to dupe Carfax—Colonel Mallinson—and sell the letters to someone else?" Cordelia asked. "Or keep them?"

"Surely Hubert Mallinson would have checked to make sure the letters were genuine before he paid," Laura said. "Maybe these are dummies in case someone tried to steal them."

They went through the rest of the coat and felt the lining. They unbuttoned his waistcoat, checked his breeches, and in the end stripped him entirely.

"I never realized how exhausting this is without the gentleman's doing any of the work," Cordelia said.

"And not particularly agreeable," Laura added, running her fingers over the waistcoat lining. "Of course, he's hardly anyone I'd have chosen to undress, with or without his cooperation." She set down the waistcoat. Mélanie did the same with his breeches.

No sign of the papers. Mélanie sat back on her heels, her

flounced golden skirts pooling about her. "I think someone else must have taken them before we could."

"And left blank dummies?" Cordelia asked. "Why?"

"Because he might have felt that his pocket was empty. This way he wouldn't notice until the meeting with Carfax. Hubert."

"Who?" Laura asked. "Who might have taken them?"

"Who not is almost a better question. Most of the people at the ball would like those letters." Mélanie pushed herself to her feet. "Better get him dressed before someone comes in, and we have a lot of explaining to do."

OUT OF THE corner of his eye, Julien saw Addison serve the doctored champagne to Sir George. And though he flattered himself a detached observer would have sworn he was looking elsewhere, a few minutes later he was aware of Cordelia's drawing Sir George onto the dance floor.

Kitty moved to his side. "Time for a distraction."

He took her hand and lifted it to his lips. Because it would draw gazes round the room. And because he liked doing it. "Oh good, there are Josefina and her family. I'm glad to see them, and this will serve nicely."

Josefina Lopes had been an agent in the Peninsula and then, like so many former agents, had settled in London after the war, where she'd become a much-fêted singer at Vauxhall Gardens. She'd married a violinist and composer and they had a young son. They lived with her parents, who had also come over from Portugal. Julien liked all of them. And Josefina's mother, like Julien's own mother, was the daughter of slaves. She had met Josefina's father, a former sailor, in Sao Tomé, where Portugal had a colony, and come back to Portugal with him. There were a number of reasons Julien felt a kinship with Josefina, but that was certainly one of them.

"Josefina." Julien leaned in to kiss her cheek. "Lucian." He shook her husband's hand and turned to her parents. "Luisa. Fernando. It's good to see you."

"It was kind of you to invite us, Lord Carfax." Josefina gave a quick smile when greetings had been exchanged. "Julien. Kitty."

"Believe me, this will lend no end of caché to our ball," Kitty said.

"Perhaps not the sort you want," Josefina said.

"On the contrary." Kitty's smile took in the whole group. "As you may have noticed, my husband has a love of creating a stir. And having the toast of Vauxhall among our guests will make us the envy of many in Mayfair. But that has nothing to do with why we wanted you here. You must bring your little boy over again soon. The children were very disappointed they wouldn't see him tonight. They don't quite see the point of a grown-up party."

"I quite agree," Josefina said.

"So do I," Julien said. "Much more rational conversation with children present." Cordelia and a wobbly Sir George had just made their way off the dance floor. The waltz that had been in progress was coming to an end. "Will you honor me with the next dance, Josefina?"

Josefina smiled. "I'd be delighted." She glanced at her husband and parents.

"I'll take care of them," Kitty said. "You must come and meet Emily Cowper. She was telling me how much she admires Lucian's music."

"You know what they'll say about our dancing together, I assume?" Josefina murmured as Julien led her onto the dance floor.

"Oh yes. I quite like the idea of everyone's being reminded of my mother and what they did to her. I hope you don't mind assisting me?"

"On the contrary."

"Trust a fellow agent to grasp the mission. You have my thanks. And I should add that any man would be honored to dance with you."

"That's just the sort of charming thing I'd expect you to say. If a bit conventional."

"I only stoop to convention when I speak the unvarnished truth."

Josefina laughed. There were indeed a number of eyes on them as they moved into the dance, but then he and Kitty had both been the center of attention all evening. As they had been for the past few months whenever they didn't go out in disguise.

But as they circled the room, he heard a woman's voice behind him say, "I suppose I shouldn't be surprised he's dancing with her. Like will find like. Though she's certainly duskier than he is."

"Doesn't change the blood that flows in his veins," a man's voice replied.

"Mallinson blood."

"And his mother's blood."

"He's still a Mallinson."

"Not sure what that means to him."

"He's undoubtedly exotic. It will be interesting to watch him."

Josefina cast a glance up at Julien. "I know a bit about what you're feeling, I think."

Julien smiled down at her as he spun her to the side. "I imagine you do."

"Not precisely, of course." Her gaze was level and friendly as she spun back to face him. "You're a Mallinson. That makes you one of them."

"I'll never be one of them." His ironic drawl, usually second nature, came out with a bite he hadn't intended.

"It may not stop the comments, but they'll always see you as a Mallinson. And an earl."

"And that gives me power. Granted."

The movement of the dance had Josefina in front of him, but she nodded. "They don't see power when they look at me. But I know how it feels to have people look at one because one's different." She spun back towards him, their hands locked overhead. "Fascinated by what seems exotic. Or repelled by it. Or often both, one after the other. Or even at the same time. But whatever they think, it's the difference they see. Not the person underneath."

Julien met her gaze. He had the unfamiliar sensation of having had his comfortable mask torn from his face. His nerve endings were exposed. "Sometimes one would just as soon they didn't see the person underneath."

Her mouth curved in a faint smile. "There is that. One can learn to play a façade to one's advantage."

"And beautiful women struggle to be seen for themselves."

"Somehow I think you also know about that, Julien."

He gave a dry laugh. "I learned early to play all the cards in my possession."

"It can certainly be an asset for an agent." She twirled beneath his arm again. "Someone asked me yesterday if I thought about going home. I said I didn't want to see Portugal with the government it has now. Then I realized she meant Sao Tomé. Where I never lived at all. Where my mother only was because her ancestors were bought and sold. My parents met there, so I suppose that gives it happy memories of a sort. But—" She looked round the ballroom. "In many ways, outsider or not, this is home."

Julien looked round the ballroom as well. The classical busts. The paintings of Mallinsons past. The Canalettos and Rubens and Van Dycks that his father had bought from Alistair Rannoch, who had obtained them through dubious means. "God help me, so it is," he said. "And now it's my children's as well."

"So I suppose it's ours to make of what we will," Josefina said.

"Well said. I abrogated my responsibilities for too long."

Josefina looked up at him as the music came to an end. "There are different ways of working for what we believe in."

"Point well taken. But far too charitable, in my case."

"I went from being an agent to being a singer at Vauxhall."

"Where your presence makes quite a statement in and of itself. Not that your agent skills couldn't be put to use." Mélanie and Laura had left the ballroom as well, dark and titian heads close together, like two friends sharing a gossip. So far, the mission was progressing as intended. "May I persuade you to another dance?"

Josefina's smile said she understood far more than she let on. "I'd be delighted, Lord Carfax."

8

"*D*arling." Mélanie found her husband near the archway to the supper room, where he was standing with Harry. "A slight problem."

Malcolm angled his head with apparent husbandly concern, as though they were exchanging a bit of familiar gossip in the midst of the ball. "You didn't get the papers?"

"Oh, we got them. At least, the papers Sir George Dalton had. I think someone else got to them first."

"Unexpected." Malcolm looked at Harry, then cast a glance round the ballroom and then into the supper room. "As we said, ninety percent of the people at the ball would want them."

"But far fewer would have the skills to take them," Harry said.

"Take what?" Julien joined them, the picture of the affable host circulating among his guests.

"Someone got to the letters before we did," Mélanie said.

"Interesting." Julien touched his champagne glass to each of theirs in turn, in a silent toast. "It's all right, anyone seeing us grouped together will just think the host is taking a moment with his friends. That's the advantage of having friends. Well, one of the advantages. I should have realized that years ago. It would have made my career as an agent easier. You should have told me."

"I hadn't realized it myself," Mélanie said. "At least, not until more recently."

"Who's the likeliest suspect?" Harry asked.

"Brougham was making noises about the letters," Malcolm said. "Which you wouldn't think he'd do if he was trying to steal them himself. Unless it was an elaborate feint. Brougham's clever enough for it. I'm not sure he has the skills to have actually stolen the letters, though. Unless he hired someone."

"Uncle Hubert might have thought he could avoid having to pay for them." Julien said. "He hasn't arrived yet, but there are a number of people he might have employed."

"How many of them are here tonight?" Harry asked.

"Quite a number of his former agents. Oliver Lydgate and Sylvie St. Ives and Maria Monreal, among others. Whether or not any of his former agents would consent to work for him is another story. We certainly worked hard enough to break away from him. But I imagine he could have found someone for the right price."

"George Dalton was in the card room before he came into the ballroom," Malcolm said.

Harry nodded. "I'll ask Archie whom he noticed Dalton talking to. Though it might have been easier to take them while he was dancing."

"Challenging to do it on the dance floor," Mélanie said. "Though not impossible. Perhaps Frances noted whom he was dancing with. We've all been watching for him all evening, but Fanny has a better eye for what's happening on the dance floor."

"What have you done with Dalton?" Harry asked.

"Dressed him again and put the dummy papers back where we found them," Mélanie said. "But when he recovers consciousness in a half hour or so, he's likely to check the papers."

"Yes, I think even Dalton has the wit for that," Harry said.

"He's likely to think you took them," Malcolm said. "Or that Cordy did, since he was with her when he passed out."

"We could have him removed," Julien suggested.

"On the contrary," Harry said. "I'll be very intrigued to see what he says to Cordy when he recovers consciousness. And if she can draw him out. I'd wager my wife is more than a match for Dalton."

KITTY MOVED out of the green salon, where some of those who didn't wish to dance had taken refuge. The "talking room," Julien called it. Now that she had left her position at the head of the stairs (a hostess was only expected to greet her guests for so long), she felt less constrained. Addison was back in his ball clothes and had been dancing with Blanca. Cordelia had left the ballroom with Sir George, and Mélanie and Laura had followed. At some point someone would update her, but there was no need to expect them to risk notice by doing so too quickly. She was glancing round the ballroom for any late arrivals she hadn't yet spoken to, when she heard a woman's high-pitched voice behind her, somehow clear as cut glass in the cacophony of voices, violin strings, and champagne glasses. "She looks genteel enough, if rather ostentatiously striking. I wasn't sure what to expect. I heard he found her in the wilds of the Argentine."

"Yes, but she was there with her first husband," said another woman's voice, less piercing but equally resonant. "Captain Ashton. So she'd had the benefit of British society. Which is more than the new Lord Carfax has had for the past five-and-twenty years."

"Blood will tell. He's a Mallinson. Whoever his mother was."

"At least he has the benefit of his mother's fortune."

"Pity that he fell into the clutches of a foreign adventuress."

"Oh, Aurelia. She's an officer's widow."

"That doesn't make her any less foreign. I couldn't bear to walk up the stairs tonight and see her standing where Amelia Carfax stood. Pamela Carfax was bad enough, but at least she seemed to know her place. The new Lady Carfax doesn't seem to understand the meaning of the word."

"How right you are," Julien said in an easy voice.

Kitty glanced over her shoulder to see that her husband had slipped through the crowd with his usual soundlessness. Two turbaned ladies stared at him in horror.

"Do leave it there," Julien said. "There's really no recovery possible. If you'll excuse me, ladies, I need to speak to my wife."

He inclined his head and took Kitty's arm. "That was very mild, for you," she said, as they moved to the side.

"Yes, well, the sort of thing I might have done in the old days would be a bit too messy in a ballroom." His hand tightened on her arm and his gaze locked on her own for a moment. "Kitkat—"

"I'm all right, Julien. It was rather amusing." She scanned his face. "Do you know anything? Do they have the papers?"

"No. Dalton had dummies on him. So someone else got to the papers first. We're trying to trace everyone who had contact with Dalton. Did you see anything?"

"No, I was at the head of the stairs most of the time." Never had she chafed at her role more.

"I'd suspect Uncle Hubert of stealing the letters to avoid buying them, but he's arriving tactfully late. Ah." Julien's gaze settled across the room. "There he is now."

Hubert Mallinson was a short man, but somehow he was instantly recognizable. Of course, it helped that at least half the people in the ballroom were looking at him as he stood just inside the door with his wife and their youngest daughter, Lucinda.

"Tactful," Kitty said. "They avoided the spectacle of greeting me on the stairs. But it's still going to be a spectacle. We should go to them and turn the spectacle as much in all our favor as possible."

9

The Mallinson family moved forwards as she and Julien approached, smiling. They all of them knew the social game. Even Lucinda, at not yet twenty.

"Good of you to invite us," Hubert said.

"Good of you to come, sir." Julien shook his uncle's hand.

"Nonsense," Amelia said, leaning forwards to accept Julien's kiss on her cheek. "We wouldn't have missed it." She looked round the room from which she had reigned over London society for two decades. "You've done a lovely job, Kitty."

"Thank you, Cousin Amelia." Kitty did not have to force the gratitude into her voice. This must be quite beastly for Amelia. "You're too kind."

"It's a statement of fact, my dear. You obviously have a knack for it."

Lucinda glanced round the ballroom. "I quite like the new wall hangings."

"That's very sweet of you, Lucy." Kitty hugged Julien's youngest cousin. "I was just about to go up and check on the children. Do you want to come with me?"

"Oh yes," Lucinda said with evident relief. "Thank you."

Lucinda glanced about with interest as they slipped through the crowd and went up the stairs to the nursery on the second floor. She dropped down on the nursery carpet with the boys and Genny just as she had in the drawing room when she first met them.

"I like that you have the nursery next to your room," she said, as she and Kitty went back downstairs. "It was the floor above when I was growing up. And it was just me and my nurse and the nursery maids much of the time, because I'm the youngest by so much."

"We're all used to being together," Kitty said. "We still feel a bit lost in such a big house." She and the children and Julien had lived in three rooms for months. Very happy months. For only part of which they'd actually been married. She paused at the stairhead, the noise from the ball drifting up about them. "I'm sure it hasn't been easy."

"Not really. I mean, it hasn't really not been easy." Lucinda fingered a fold of her cornflower gauze skirt. "I mean, things have been unsettled between Papa and Mama for a bit, but that was going on long before this. I always liked the Grange better than Carfax Court. Papa seems happy there. Our new house in London is fine. My favorite thing about Carfax House was always sliding down the banisters, and I'm too old for that now." She touched her finger to the polished mahogany stair rail with a faintly wistful look. "In a way, it's easier to have people fuss about me less. Though Mama seems more worried than ever about my finding a husband. It's not as though I don't have a dowry. I needn't marry at all, if I don't wish to."

"Certainly not." Kitty smiled at Julien's cousin. "Though I can say from experience that when one finds the right person, it can be very much worth it. And I speak as someone who was quite sure I wouldn't marry again."

"Well, yes, that's different. I should think it would entirely be worth it if one fell in love that much. As much as you and

Julien." She glanced back towards the nursery. "And I can quite see wanting children—sometime."

"It's not for everyone," Kitty said. "For a long time, I thought it wasn't for me. But now—I wouldn't have missed it for anything. And I thought that, even when I thought I didn't want another husband. But I'm rather glad I didn't do it when I was younger."

"I suppose you're used to being at the center of things."

"Not like this."

"It's not so hard." Lucinda glanced down the stairs as the noise of the party wafted up at them. "Just tiresome, at times, but you won't need to take it so seriously. I'm sure you'll do splendidly."

"Thank you, sweetheart. But I'm not even sure what that means."

~

"DAVENPORT."

Harry Davenport stopped in his perambulation about the room. He'd been attempting to look nonchalant while keeping an eye out for George Dalton to return to the ballroom. He had ascertained that his Uncle Archie hadn't seen any opportunity for anyone to get the papers off Dalton in the card room while Archie had been present, and had left Archie to keep an eye on the card room. No one would be surprised to find Archie there all evening—at least, not the man Archie had been before he'd married Malcolm's aunt Frances two years ago. But if Harry stayed too long among the baize-covered tables it might raise questions. So he'd returned to the ballroom. Where he now found himself looking at Thomas Thornsby, his fellow Classicists' Society member, whose brother Lewis's death had been the subject of their investigation the previous January.

"Thornsby." Harry took a sip from the glass of port he'd acquired in the card room. "I'm glad you came."

"It was kind of the Carfaxes to extend the invitation." Thomas glanced round the room. Harry saw his gaze settle on Edith Simmons, a fellow classicist, who since last January's investigation made her home with Harry and Cordelia. Edith was talking with Sandy Trenor and Bet Simcox and some other young people close to her age. Laughing in a way she hadn't been able to at public gatherings in her role as governess. "It's good to see Edith able to go out in society."

"The life of a governess is damnable," Harry said with genuine feeling. "I'm glad she can escape its strictures. Though she seems quite engaged by the plans for the school."

"The one you're opening with the Rannochs."

"We've contributed. The Rannochs are giving one of their properties for it. The O'Roarkes are involved as well. In fact, Mrs. O'Roarke is leading the project. She has a lot of ideas from being a governess herself and teaching our children. They're thinking of having a branch in London, so children don't have to be away from their parents."

Thomas nodded, as though trying to focus on something other than Edith. "It's a girls' school?"

"Girls and boys. Laura's quite determined they do lessons together. It's for children who can't get a good education other-wise. Of course, we can't reach half of those who could really use it."

"It's a noble enterprise."

"It's an attempt to do something. Which helps us all sleep better at night. I hope it at least does the same for the pupils."

Thomas gave a faint smile. "You have a hard time admitting to your own kindness, Davenport."

"I'm all for kindness, but a few acts of kindness can't fix the ills of the world."

"They can make a world of difference for individual people,

though. It's very good of you and Lady Cordelia to have taken Edith in."

"We're very fond of Edith. The girls are fond of her."

Thomas's gaze settled on Edith across the ballroom again. "She looks happy."

"I think she's enjoying stretching her wings." Harry cast a sidelong look at Thomas. "I also think she misses you."

Thomas tore his gaze away. "There's been a great deal to do in the family. I've seen her at the Classicists' Society. And at your house. You know that. But I can't—"

"You've had a lot to adjust to."

Thomas stared into the depths of his glass. If it weren't for lack of fortune on both sides, Harry was quite sure Thomas would have offered for Edith a long time since. But challenging as their lack of fortune was, the gulf between them was more complicated. In January, Thomas had learned that Edith had been blackmailed by Lady Shroppington, Thomas's great-aunt, into spying for the Elsinore League. Including spying on Thomas. "I understand why Edith did what she did," Thomas said in a low, unusually rough voice. "God knows I understand protecting one's family. All too keenly. I honor her for it. Of course, it's made me look at a number of things differently. But it hasn't changed—essentials."

"That's the important thing, surely."

Thomas dragged his gaze back to Harry's face. "You've never wanted for fortune, Davenport. I have to figure out how I'm going to provide for my sisters, and look after my parents. It's quite clear we can expect nothing from Aunt Henrietta." He paused and drew a hard breath. "Not that I'd take it from her if she offered."

"You need a wife with a fortune."

Thomas grimaced. "Even if I could make things work, I haven't a great deal to offer Edith. Oh, perhaps I do a bit, compared to what she had as a governess, but look at her now." He watched Edith step into a waltz with Sandy Trenor.

"Trenor's madly in love with his charming mistress," Harry said. Bet Simcox was dancing with Benedict Smythe and clearly unconcerned about Sandy's affections.

"Not that. Not Trenor, necessarily. The circles she's moving in now. She'll meet a score of men who could offer her a great deal more."

"She may not want a great deal more. Of course, she may not want to be married at all."

Thomas met Harry's gaze without surprise. "Yes, I know Edith's views on marriage. I'm not so stodgy I don't understand them. I think she might change her mind for the right man."

"So do I. Assuming the man had the sense to not expect her to be anyone other than who she is. But then, you've always struck me as eminently sensible."

Thomas gave a twisted smile. "You're a romantic, Davenport."

"Ha."

Thomas looked at Edith again, as she and Trenor circled by. "Is she safe?"

Harry felt the sardonic smile leave his face. "We've been watching closely, but we've had no intelligence to suggest she isn't. Lady Shroppington has other matters to deal with."

"But—"

"We'll continue to watch."

Thomas shook his head. "I can't make sense of my aunt."

"Nor can any of us."

Thomas stared into his champagne glass, as though searching for answers in the depths. "We've seen Aunt Henrietta a few times. Father won't forbid her the house, and for a number of reasons I think it's prudent not to do so. But I can scarcely hold my tongue round her. In truth, at first I thought I wouldn't even be able to look her in the eye. But it's amazing how the training of social civility holds one."

"Anything you can learn from her could be of great help," Harry said.

Thomas met his gaze. "That's the only reason I can stomach talking to her. But she hasn't revealed anything so far. I'm stunned she can sit at my parents' table and look us all in the eye, and share our food, and drink our wine."

"She wanted Edith to uncover information on you,' Harry said. "It would be invaluable to know what. And why. But not if it means putting yourself at risk."

"Aren't we all at risk until she's stopped?" Thomas's voice went unexpectedly hard.

"Point taken. But you're sensible enough to draw the line at things you shouldn't do without an agent's training."

Thomas looked at Edith. She was laughing up at Trenor as she twirled, a bit awkwardly, under his arm. Simply in friendship, with no attempt at flirtation, but her expression was still intoxicating. "I don't feel very sensible just now. I feel the distinct desire to take action."

Harry touched his friend's shoulder. "Understandable. But you're too sensible to do so foolishly." He made it as much warning as statement.

Thomas's answering nod was not as reassuring as Harry would have liked.

I O

—————

*E*dith Simmons left the dance floor on Sandy Trenor's arm, and went still as the stir of movement from couples leaving the floor gave her a sudden view of a familiar figure across the room. For a moment her delightfully impractical satin dancing slippers seemed stuck to the floorboards. Thomas Thornsby's gaze locked on her own, or at least it seemed that way. He inclined his head. How could one attempt to read so much into a simple nod? Edith nodded back just before a sea of dancers in gauzy pastel frocks and sleek dark coats blurred the distance between them. Should she cross the room and speak with him, or wait and let him make the decision? After all, in a sense he was the injured party. Well, he certainly was; she'd been spying on him, and polite as he was, there was certainly a restraint in his manner that hadn't been present before January. Difficult to tell how much was because of her actions and how much because of the impossibility of anything's developing between them. Thomas was so faultlessly well-mannered it was difficult to tell anything.

"Miss Simmons?" Sandy asked. "Did you see someone you know? Shall we cross the room?"

"No. Yes. That is, I'm not sure—"

"Edith."

The familiar voice sounded from one side, taking Edith back to another part of her past that was inextricably bound up with Thomas and her time as a reluctant agent of the Elsinore League. She turned and found herself looking at the woman who had employed her five months since. Alice Wilton. Lady Wilton. She had been a kind mistress and a good mother, if more detached from both the nursery and the nursery staff than the Rannochs and the Davenports. And the new Carfaxes, from everything Edith had seen.

"Lady Wilton." Edith smiled, unsure if she should curtsey or shake hands, and convinced she'd make a mull of either. "I believe you're acquainted with Mr. Trenor?"

"Lady Wilton." Sandy, who also had beautiful manners, sketched a faultless bow. They exchanged pleasantries. Sandy looked between the two women and met Edith's gaze with the faintest lift of his brow, which managed to question if she was comfortable being left alone with her acquaintance. Edith inclined her head. She wasn't sure why Lady Wilton had sought her out, but she sensed the other woman needed to talk.

Sandy gave a quick smile. "If you'll excuse me, ladies, I should see how Miss Simcox is getting on."

Edith met Lady Wilton's gaze. She had once lived in the other woman's household, but she had had relatively few conversations with her, and certainly not at occasions such as a ball where they were both guests and on equal footing. "How are Winston and Sally?" she asked.

"They're well." A smile broke the well-bred composure on Lady Wilton's face, though concern lurked in her eyes. "They've been asking to meet you in the park again with the Davenport girls."

"I'd like that. I'm sure Livia and Drusilla would as well."

Though last time, Lady Wilton had stayed and Edith had had to make small talk and hadn't been able to romp with the children as she'd have liked. Perhaps she could bring Cordelia with her next time to distract Lady Wilton…

"Oh, good." Lady Wilton gave a strained smile, and for the oddest moment, Edith had a sense that the other woman wished she could unbend more than she did. "Edith—" Lady Wilton fingered the sticks of her fan. "I know the Davenports investigate things with the Rannochs. That is, crimes. Or—"

"Yes, they're quite brilliant at it." Edith peered at her former employer. "Lady Wilton? Is there something you need investigated?'

"Me?" She jerked her hand back from the fan. "Goodness, no, why should I—Oh, dear, Edith, can we talk?"

Edith glanced round the ballroom. She could hardly claim to know Carfax House well, but she had been to dine with the Davenports once or twice and different as the house looked filled with flowers and ball guests, she had a rough sense of the geography. She inclined her head to the left and led Lady Wilton down a passage to an anteroom hung with ecru watered silk that was larger than her own parents' drawing room. The room was empty, though the lamps had been lit and crystal bowls of the same beautiful peach roses that adorned the ballroom stood on the mantel and the polished tables.

Lady Wilton crossed the room and turned to face Edith, gloved hands clasped together, face a study in conflict. She was a tall woman, nearly as tall as Edith herself, though she seemed much more at home in her blue satin evening gown and long white gloves than Edith could ever imagine feeling in her own evening dress. As though she had been born with the knack of holding a fan and champagne glass in gloved fingers, and not letting her shawl slip indecorously from her shoulders. Her dark blonde hair was dressed with its usual elegance. But her eyes held a desperation Edith had never before seen on her former mistress's well-bred face.

"I don't quite know how to tell you this."

"You needn't fear I'll tell anyone." Edith took a step forwards, then paused, aware her skirt was tangled about her legs and her shawl was dangling from one arm. "I mean—I wouldn't."

"No, you wouldn't." Lady Wilton's face softened into a smile, though the strain didn't leave her eyes. "Toby—Sir Tobias—was stationed in Italy for a time. You know that."

"Yes." Sally and Winston had often talked about their Italian adventures.

Lady Wilton gave a quick nod. "While we were abroad, we were sometimes in attendance upon the Princess of Wales. That is, Queen Caroline."

"That must be awkward now." Edith tugged her shawl up. It slithered off her other arm. "I mean, with Sir Toby's working for the government."

"Yes. I hardly suspected—the thing is, I wrote some letters at the time. Only statements of the truth of what I saw when we spent time with the princess. It never occurred to me what importance might be laid on simple expressions of the truth."

"I imagine a number of people must have questions for you now." Edith grabbed the loose end of the shawl. It was red and black Italian silk, a beloved birthday gift from the Davenports, but it seemed to slide the moment it touched the silk of her gown. "And be asking you for your letters."

"Yes." Lady Wilton closed her hands together. "The thing is, I no longer have the letters. I wrote them to a gentleman we met in Italy."

Edith's fingers froze on the shawl as she began to see the risk. "And he's given them to someone to make use of?"

"No, he can't. That is—" Lady Wilton's fingers locked tighter. "He's no longer alive."

"Good God," Edith was startled into saying. "I'm so sorry."

"Yes, you know him, or know of him. Mr. Lewis Thornsby."

Edith stared at her former employer. She was growing used to the way things were interconnected in her world. Or rather, the world she had stumbled into, a world of spies and double agents, secret societies, and tangled family connections. But the idea that Lady Wilton had been acquainted with Thomas's brother Lewis, who had been murdered at the Tavistock Theatre on the orders of their great aunt, Lady Shroppington, who in turn had set Edith herself to spy on the Wiltons, shook her to the core. "I had no idea you knew him."

"No." Lady Wilton tugged at a ringlet that had tangled round her diamond earring. "He didn't call on us in London. It was quite a casual acquaintance. At least, as far as my husband knew."

Edith sometimes felt she was very slow at these things, but she began to sense where they were headed. "But you and Mr. Thornsby formed a closer friendship."

"Yes." Lady Wilton kept her gaze steady, though her cheeks colored beneath her delicately applied rouge. "We were—he was kind to me. At a time when I needed kindness."

Sir Toby was a conscientious man, much devoted to his work. Lady Wilton was an admirable hostess and the relation-ship seemed placid. But hardly passionate, in Edith's view. Not that she was much equipped to judge passion. "The letters you wrote to Mr. Thornsby—"

"Have fallen into other hands." Lady Wilton's fingers tight-ened on the folds of her gown. "I'm not sure how. I can only assume they were discovered after his death. Mr. Thornsby was —a good friend. I don't think he'd have betrayed me."

"No, of course not," Edith said, though after the investigation into Thornsby's murder, she was not quite so sanguine.

"The letters have apparently been offered up for sale. They

are of interest because of the information they contain about Princess Caroline—the queen. But of course, if the letters become public, my secrets will be revealed as well. And I fear Sir Toby would not understand."

"I quite see that." The shawl fell on the floor again. Edith bunched it up and tossed it onto a chair covered in cream watered silk. "Do you know where the letters are now?"

"They're to be exchanged—sold—at the ball tonight."

"And you thought—"

"Colonel Davenport used to be an agent. He and Lady Cordelia investigate with the Rannochs. I hoped—"

"You want me to tell them."

Lady Wilton drew a breath like breaking glass. "I don't want anyone else to know. But I think they're my only hope of getting the letters back. So you'll have to tell them. I know how much it is to ask. But it would be so dreadful, not just for me, but for Sally and Winston. For their sake—"

"Of course. I hate the thought of anyone's private life being toyed with. I'll do everything I can."

"You're too good, Edith." Lady Wilton drew the pale blue folds of her own shawl up about her shoulders. "You must despise me."

"Nonsense." Edith was already moving to the door, but she turned back. "Whom you love is your own affair. I've never been married, and I don't know that I want to be—it rather terrifies me, for a number for reasons. But I imagine it's fiendishly difficult."

A faint smile, half regret, half perhaps remembered happiness, shot across Lady Wilton's face. "Not all the time. And in the right circumstances it can be quite splendid. But it can also be awkward. One can—grow apart. Without an open quarrel, without even realizing it's happening. Sometimes it can be mended. I'm not sure, in our case. But at least, I hope to avoid an irrevocable break. That would be too beastly for the children."

Who would be likely to lose their mother, the way the law worked. In a divorce or even a legal separation, the children almost always stayed with the father "I'll everything I can," Edith said, and left the room to find Cordelia as quickly as possible.

"Cordy." Edith found her friend navigating the tables in the supper room, where guests were beginning to gather, and caught her arm.

"Edith. I'm so glad to see you enjoying yourself." Cordelia's quick smile gave way to a look of concern. "Goodness, what's the matter? Has a gentleman been difficult?"

"No, nothing like that. I'd know how to handle that on my own. But something *is* the matter. In fact, it's quite beastly." Edith drew Cordelia between the tables to the edge of the room near the French windows. It was only then that she realized Cordelia had an abstracted expression herself. "Is something wrong?" Edith asked.

"No. That is, nothing to stop you from telling me what concerns you."

Edith cast a quick glance round, though she was enough of a spy now herself to know the buzz of conversation afforded good cover. She told Cordelia about her conversation with Lady Wilton, and the letters.

Cordelia's brows drew together. "This does complicate things."

"Complicate?" Edith scanned Cordelia's face. She looked less shocked than like someone putting pieces together. "You mean you knew—"

"About the letters. Not that they were Lady Wilton's. But we're already doing our best to get them back."

"Do you know who has them?"

Cordelia sighed. "We thought we did. But it's all got a bit more complicated."

CARFAX—HUBERT Mallinson—took a drink of champagne. "Good vintage."

"You bought it," Julien told his uncle. "Though there was port in the cellar my father laid down."

"Let me guess. You poured it out."

"I was going to, but Kitty pointed out it was a sad waste. We sent it to some friends in St. Giles who will appreciate it." Julien brushed a speck of lint from his lapel. "I poured the rum out."

Hubert gave a curt nod, no surprise in his gaze. "Your speech was impressive," he said without preamble, though it really wasn't such a leap from the rum to Julien's abolition speech.

"You're generous, Uncle Hubert."

Hubert glanced at his wife, who was speaking with the Castlereaghs. "We both know I'm nothing of the sort. You've made a mark for yourself. I don't actually disagree with much of what you said. Practically, it can't be accomplished now, though."

"Can't be, or won't be, because people don't think it's worth the effort?"

Hubert raised a brow. "You'd be uprooting our colonies."

"Not necessarily a bad thing. Some of them have already uprooted themselves. Not that that's helped the slaves in their new country that's supposedly founded on life, liberty, and the pursuit of happiness. You heard I affirmed the freedom of the Carfax slaves?"

"I thought you would." Carfax adjusted his spectacles. "I wasn't pleased to become a slave owner, you know."

Julien took a drink of champagne. "And yet you remained one."

"Unlike you, I wasn't willing to let my investment fall apart. I could have sold the plantation and said my hands were clean, but a new master might have been worse. And if I'd sold the plantation and the slaves, you wouldn't have been able to free them."

"That's a damnable excuse for inactivity, Uncle Hubert."

"It's a practical excuse."

"You could, of course, have freed the slaves yourself."

"It wasn't the time for such an extravagant gesture."

Julien turned, shoulders pressed against the column behind him. "And when, precisely, will it be the time?"

"Sooner than many think. The Spanish and French and India could provide cheaper sugar if it weren't for tariffs. The plantations aren't sustainable long term."

"And commerce, of course, is what drives humanity."

"You're enough of a pragmatist to see that, Julien. Now that slavery is a source of instability, it's untenable."

"One reason among many I don't regret the *Unicorn* Rebellion. It contributed to the instability."

Hubert gave a grunt of acknowledgement. "The world is changing. Whether I like it or not. But you can't push it too fast."

"And so we tell people in chains to wait?"

"You're starting to sound like Malcolm."

"Thank you. That's the most complimentary thing anyone's said to me in an age."

"You aren't blinded by your ideals, Julien."

"If you're saying Malcolm is, perhaps the world would be a better place if we were all so blinded."

"Don't be clever."

"For once, I'm not trying to be." Julian regarded his uncle. "This is all about change. Some of us are trying to figure out the most effective way to bring it about. You're trying to stop it."

Hubert looked from the stucco ceiling to the French windows. "You're going to bring all this tumbling about your ears if you have your way."

"Perhaps it should come tumbling down. But I don't think it will."

"I'd hoped—"

"That being Carfax would make me take it seriously? I take seriously anyone I'm responsible for. But as to the name and property—I don't think I'll ever see property as you do. But perhaps being the grandson of someone who was considered property has left an indelible stamp on me."

Hubert hesitated for the barest fraction of a second. "Don't be dramatic, Julien. You don't believe bloodlines change you. That's the sort of thing your enemies say."

"I don't think my blood makes me any different from anyone else. I do think the way my ancestors were treated has impacted who I am. You should understand. You have a great deal of respect for the past."

"The past teaches us valuable lessons. But you can't live in it and nor can the rest of us. The future doesn't lie in the West Indies. It lies in India."

"You should talk to Laura O'Roarke. She'd point out just how untenable our behavior in India is."

Hubert took another sip of champagne. "India will ensure the supremacy of the British for generations to come."

"Until the Indians decide they won't put up with it. There are a lot more of them than of us."

Hubert raised a brow. "We have the guns. You should appreciate that."

"Guns can change hands. You should appreciate that." Julien

regarded his uncle for a moment. "You believe in stability. Above all things, it often seems. There's precious little stability in being dependent on an oppressed majority. Whether or not they're technically called slaves."

"My God, Julien. I used to be able to at least depend on you for healthy cynicism."

"You think recognizing the power imbalance in the world isn't cynical?"

"Phrased as a call to uprising?" Hubert tugged a cuff smooth. "Yes. You make the mistake of thinking the masses are as rational as you are."

"Oh, I don't think I'm in the least rational. But I do think giving all of us in our irrationality an equal say is the best solution."

Hubert gave a grunt of incredulity. "You've lost your sense, Julien. Even your Bonaparte didn't believe that."

"Oh, not in the least. But he was hardly my Bonaparte. Even his wife wasn't my Josephine, though I did share her bed. Let me get you some more champagne."

élanie looked at Cordelia as she finished explaining about Alice Wilton and the letters. "Well, this changes things. Though it was always going to be an issue."

Malcolm shot a look at her.

Mélanie looked at her husband. "I may not have as finely tuned scruples as you, darling, but I knew we'd have to examine the letters and see how much damage they could do, whoever had written them, before we decided what to do with them. I certainly want to help the queen's cause, but someone's life and reputation are at stake."

Malcolm nodded.

"It shouldn't make a difference that it's someone we know," Cordelia said. "But it does put it in perspective."

They were on the balcony, gathered together at the rail. Others had sought refuge on the balcony, especially couples seeking a quiet moment, but leaning over the gilded rail, they could easily appear to simply be admiring the colored lanterns Mélanie and Cordelia had helped choose to hang in the garden below. Strains of music sounded from the ballroom behind them. Colored lights danced below, illuminating more guests who had gone out into the garden. An occasional laugh or flirtatious giggle floated up on the breeze.

"Interesting it was Thornsby who had the letters," Malcolm said. "I wonder if the League managed to get them from his things after he was killed, despite our efforts. Or if he turned them over long before."

"And if the League suggested he have an affair with Alice Wilton," Mélanie said.

Malcolm met her gaze. "Quite."

"You think Lady Shroppington—or, at least, her faction in the League—were orchestrating this from the beginning?" Cordelia asked.

"Information about Princess Caroline—the queen—has been valuable for a long time," Malcolm said. "A good strategist—which Lady Shroppington certainly is—could have seen ahead to where we are now. If she knew Alice Wilton was friendly with the queen, it would have made sense for her to suggest Lewis get close to Lady Wilton. And it also might explain setting Edith to spy on the Wiltons."

"It doesn't change the immediate objective," Mélanie said. "We have to figure out who has the letters now. And get them back—even if it's someone on our side when it comes to the queen."

"Dalton could wake up at any moment now," Cordelia said. "I'm rather looking forward to confronting him."

"Has anyone told Raoul the letters were dummies?" Mélanie asked. "I haven't seen him since before we took the fake letters off Dalton."

Malcolm frowned. "Nor have I."

~

RAOUL SLIPPED into an anteroom hung with pale blue silk. Not the first time he'd had a secret meeting in this room. It was conveniently small, and yet one could slip into it through the enfiladed reception rooms without drawing attention by going down the first-floor passage.

The woman he had come to meet was sitting in the shadows, leaning back in her chair as though she had escaped the ball with a headache. She might be little more than twenty, but her instincts were superb. At his entrance, she cast a glance up, then seeing it was he, pushed herself to her feet and stepped forwards. "I don't think anyone saw me."

"I'm quite sure they didn't. You're very good at this."

Sofia Montagu smiled, though her gaze remained level. "I'm still a novice compared to most of our friends."

When Raoul first met Sofia during their stay at Lake Como two years ago, she'd been scarcely out of the schoolroom, but even then she'd been working for the Carbonari and had managed to break the Elsinore League's formidable codes. Raoul pulled a sealed paper from inside his coat. "This bank draft should allow the necessary funds to be transferred. I've already moved assets to Italy."

Sofia took the paper and inclined her head. "You know how much Metternich has papers searched in Lombardy. But the Carbonari have excellent channels for avoiding his agents. I use them myself for communicating with my mother and Uncle Bernard, so no one will be suspicious when I send this." She looked into Raoul's eyes. "This has to remain secret."

"I understand."

Sofia tucked the paper into the bodice of her gown without embarrassment but with care, as though perhaps trying not to dislodge her corset laces. Raoul glanced tactfully away. "You don't want Malcolm to know," Sofia said. "That makes sense. But I also don't want Kit to know. It could hurt his relationship with his father."

Raoul nodded. Sofia and Kit Montagu had been married less than six months, after a long betrothal and a great deal of time separated, with him in Britain and her in Italy. "I appreciate your running the risk."

"I'm more pragmatic about these things than Kit is. And in some ways, I know Uncle Bernard better." She hesitated. Uncle Bernard was Lord Thurston, Kit's father, who had run off to Italy over fifteen years ago to live with Sofia's mother. And who supported his two families by dealing in guns. Some of which Raoul was buying for his agents in Spain. "I know Uncle Bernard isn't a Radical. I know he arms all sides. But he takes his promises seriously. I don't think he'll betray you. But you should be cautious."

Raoul smiled. "Believe me, I always am."

Her gaze was clear and steady. "It's different for Kit. He hasn't seen fighting. Not the sort you have. Not the sort I grew up with. It changes one. It changes the calculations. It's all less theoretical."

"Sofia—" Raoul hesitated, looking down at her young, determined face, oddly reminded of Mélanie in their days in Spain. "You and Kit are just starting out. You want to have a care for your marriage."

Sofia laughed, though her eyes had gone worldly-wise beyond her years. "Does any of us really have the luxury of doing that?"

"It's always a balancing act. But you have a chance to strike a good balance."

She adjusted her shawl. "We're doing the best we can. Isn't that all we can do, as you would say?"

"Yes. But one has to weigh the risks against the rewards. Some prices are too high to pay."

"So there are things you wouldn't do because of your marriage?"

"Oh, yes. Though that doesn't mean my marriage is safe. Or that I haven't run incalculable risks with it."

"Well, then. Kit and I married knowing we both want to change the world. Neither of us has illusions."

"My dear Sofia." Raoul touched her hand. "Perhaps the most dangerous illusion of all is the illusion that one doesn't have illusions."

1 3

"*L*ord Palmerston." Kitty smiled at the secretary at war, whom she had made a concerted effort to cultivate as part of her strategy for building support for Spain. Less than a year ago, she hadn't been quite sure how far that cultivation would go.

"Lady Carfax." Palmerston bowed over her hand. "You've done a remarkable job with the house."

"We haven't really changed it that much." In truth, she'd been far too busy to have much time for it. How had Mélanie managed?

"The mood is quite different. If I may so as a bachelor, it feels more like a family home."

"Thank you." Kitty gave an unforced smile. "That's a great compliment."

"It's the truth. Few enough houses in Mayfair have that feeling. Especially houses built on this scale."

Kitty glanced round the yellow salon, the second enfiladed salon to open off the ballroom. When they weren't entertaining, the boys liked to run races up and down the enfilade, with Genny toddling after. "It's nowhere I ever imagined living."

"Life can take one unexpected places. Your husband said that when I saw him in Westminster. I look forward to working with him."

"I'm sure he looks forward to working with you." She wasn't entirely just being a good political wife as she said it. Julien had described Palmerston as surprisingly sensible for a Tory. Which was high praise from Julien.

"I suspect you've been a great influence on him."

"We both came to the marriage with very strong ideas. But one might say we've influenced each other." Kitty kept her gaze on Palmerston, but she was aware of Raoul slipping through the crowd. In a seemingly aimless way perhaps only another agent would have recognized as purposeful. Following a clue about the missing papers? Did he know Dalton had had dummies on him? She'd been looking for him to tell him so when Palmerston waylaid her.

Palmerston smiled. "You needn't worry; I have no illusions your husband will be an ally of the Tories. He's already made quite a name for himself. In private, at least, I can tell you I admire much of what he said on abolition."

"Many people have said so. And yet nothing seems to change." Kitty fixed Palmerston with a direct gaze. Really, he was too sensible for his political party.

Palmerston had the grace to look abashed. "It's a complicated issue. It tangles with many things."

"Including finances. Including the finances of many people in this room." She hadn't used to be so blunt. She'd been accustomed to tempering her words to the end she was trying to achieve. Tactics mattered more than grand statements. And yet she found it harder to keep silent these days. At least, in some cases. Perhaps Julien had influenced her more than she realized. Which was odd in and of itself, and odd because he had scarcely seemed a font of Radical thought. But then, so much about Julien had always been masked.

"Things will change," Palmerston said. "The slave trade was abolished. Slaves will be emancipated eventually. We have to be patient."

"Easy enough to be patient here." Kitty glanced at the yellow watered-silk hangings and Robert Adam fireplace. "Rather harder to tell the slaves cutting sugar cane to make the sugar in our tea. Or an enslaved mother who knows her child won't be free and could be sold away from her."

"I begin to think you pen your husband's speeches, as Mélanie Rannoch does."

"Neither of us does so entirely. We both offer advice." Out of the corner of her eye she saw Raoul go through the door to the antechamber that opened off the salon. Not surprising, necessarily, save that about ten minutes before, when she and Lucinda came downstairs, she had seen Sofia Montagu go through the other door to the antechamber that opened off the first-floor passage. "Mélanie and Malcolm both gave Julien advice as well."

"Yes, so I suspected, listening to your husband's excellent maiden speech. It's quite a change in the Mallinson family."

"It's a change in the possessor of the Carfax title. My husband and his cousin David are in agreement in a number of areas."

"For a self-proclaimed independent who says he'll always be on the fringe, Malcolm Rannoch has gathered quite a powerful group round him."

"Surely you're far too astute to be surprised by anything Malcolm Rannoch does."

Palmerston grinned. "You'd think I would be. He's been taking us by surprise since he was at Harrow. Not least when he married Mélanie. And he's always far more in command of a situation than he admits."

"Precisely."

His grin deepened. "You and your husband are going to shake up Westminster. Which is a very good thing."

"Are you so sure of that? You're a member of the government, after all."

"Hardly a senior member And surely you realize one does not always agree with one's colleagues."

"Well put, Lord Palmerston."

He lifted his glass to her in acknowledgement and took a drink of champagne. "I take it your interest in Spain hasn't lessened due to your marriage and your husband's interests?"

"By no means. A tyrannical government may not be quite the equal of slavery, but at the root it is still a matter of freedom."

His gaze narrowed. "Is that what you'd call the Bourbon government in Spain? Tyrannical?"

"My dear Lord Palmerston. Even as a Tory, you're too sensible to call the Bourbon government in Spain—or the one in France, for that matter—anything else."

"Perhaps not. Unofficially."

"Of course, Mary Wollstonecraft compared marriage to slavery. And, certainly, the law gives husbands the power to be tyrants, if they choose to exercise it."

"And yet you've risked the dangerous institution of marriage twice."

"The first time, one could say I was too young to know better." That wasn't entirely true, but given the exigencies of the war, it had seemed the best choice. "I never thought I'd risk it again. My husband is a quite remarkable man."

"I suspect you're right. He's certainly a very fortunate man."

"I'm a fortunate woman. Or perhaps we're both fortunate, in that I doubt there are many who could put up with either of us."

"Rannoch."

"Trenchard." Malcolm, who had been looking for Raoul and keeping an eye out for George Dalton to reappear, shook hands with Laura's brother-in-law. "I'm glad you and Hetty could come."

"Of course. The Carfaxes are family, one way and another." James, Duke of Trenchard, cast a glance about the ballroom. "I won't deny it's odd. I remember coming here when I was a boy and Father had just married Mary." His gaze focused on his late father's second wife in the crowd, now holding the arm of her current husband, Gui Laclos. "Mary seems comfortable with the situation."

Malcolm could remember a time when being an earl's eldest daughter had been an intrinsic part of Mary Mallinson's identity. But between marrying a duke and finding it was not what she had anticipated, and then falling in love with and marrying a French émigré of indeterminant heritage, Mary had changed a great deal. "I think she is."

Trenchard nodded. "She seems more content these days. Though I suppose it's not surprising that anyone would have been discontented, married to Father. Laclos's a good man, and a good father to the children."

One of whom was in fact Gui Laclos's child, not the Duke of Trenchard's. Not for the first time, Malcolm wondered if James knew or guessed. James was the sort who wouldn't let on, even if he did. "Yes, he is," Malcolm said. "And he and Mary are very much in love."

James gave a quick smile. Reticent as he was about his emotions, he was also very much in love with his own wife. "That helps." His smile deepened as they watched Mary take her husband's hand and draw him onto the dance floor. Then his gaze moved to Mary's father. "And Carfax—that is, Colonel Mallinson—looks fairly contented."

"He could also hardly be otherwise."

James shot a sharp look at Malcolm.

"His nephew has returned from the dead. How could he not appear pleased?"

James gave a slow smile. "You have a wicked tongue, Rannoch."

"At times."

James's gaze moved to Julien, who was speaking to Lord Liverpool, the prime minister. "I heard his maiden speech. He has a powerful style. And he's made it clear he's a force to be reckoned with."

Malcolm met James's gaze. James was a Tory, and though Malcolm liked and respected him, they were opposed on most issues. They had never discussed slavery, however. "I think that was his intention."

"And his intention with tonight's event, I imagine." James watched Julien and Liverpool a moment longer. "My father disliked Liverpool, as you know. Rather intensely. Partly because of a past disagreement over a young woman, but also because Liverpool is part Indian."

It was something the prime minister made no effort to hide. "Yes, I know." Malcolm kept his voice even. He believed passionately in tolerance and trying to understand one's foe, but he'd be hard-pressed not to plant the former Duke of Trenchard a facer should the man suddenly rise from the dead, as Arthur Mallinson had done.

"I can only imagine what he'd make of the new Lord Carfax, for any number of reasons." James's gaze remained on Julien. "Slavery's an ugly business. It needs to go. I could imagine making common cause with Carfax"—He frowned—"I can't get used to saying that."

"None of us can."

"Yes, well, I could imagine making common cause with him over abolition. But when it comes to other things—how Radical is he?"

"Probably not more so than I am. How much does that scare you?"

James grinned. "You know how I respect you, Rannoch. It's no secret I often don't agree with you, but you make me think. Carfax is a bit different, though. He's in the Lords. I know some would say the real business gets done in the Commons, but Carfax represents a powerful estate. Part of the foundation of the country."

"You're starting to sound like the former Lord Carfax."

"I disagree with him on a number of things. But we share an appreciation of the dangers of instability."

"Questions of justice aside, stability can be so inflexible it brings the world tumbling down about one's ears."

James frowned. "You can't be blind to the unrest gripping the country."

"And our current government is a model of inflexible stability."

"You think we're on the verge of a revolution?"

"No, more's the pity."

"You don't really mean that, Rannoch."

"I believe we desperately need change. I believe in change through legal channels. But it often takes illegal actions to start that change. And don't forget the French Revolution began in the Assembly. Just as the Civil War began in Parliament."

1 4

*K*itty excused herself to Palmerston and went back into the passage. A short time later, she saw Raoul emerge from the antechamber. She hesitated. By any measure, there was a great deal going on tonight. Still, this was not something she could afford to let go. For any number of reasons. She slipped down the passage, smiling at her guests, and fell into step beside him. "You aren't dancing."

"I'm a bit old for that, don't you think?"

"Nonsense. I've seen you dance with your wife. Most women would give a great deal for a partner of such skill who looked at them in that way. On the other hand, there's always work agents find more suited to antechambers." Kitty took two glasses of champagne from a passing footman and gave one to him. "I know you were speaking with Sofia," she said, lifting her glass to his. "You did an excellent job slipping through the various rooms, but I saw both of you, and I've lived here long enough now to know how convenient that antechamber is for secret meetings. And from talk I've heard among Spanish émigrés, I know or can hazard a shrewd guess why you were meeting."

"Ah." Raoul pressed his glass to hers and took a sip.

Kitty tucked her arm through his and drew him to the side, a hostess sharing a quiet moment with an old friend. "You didn't tell me about it."

"My dear Kitty." He smiled at her as though they were two friends sharing a joke. "I couldn't do that to you tonight."

"You didn't used to believe in such niceties."

"My dear girl. We've all changed. I may be slow, but I hope I've learned some things."

Kitty leaned against the wall, head angled, so her words went straight to him. "I won't let my husband wrap me in cotton wool. You can't think I'd let you do so."

"Oh, well." Raoul grinned. "One tends to be much harder on a husband. Laura wouldn't put up with it from me, either."

"Well, then."

"Kitty." His gaze settled on her face, sharp as the sword she'd seen him wield with lethal skill and yet at the same time disconcertingly open. "Tonight is important. For you. For Julien. For his work in Parliament. For what you're planning in Spain."

"Which is why we should be allies."

He took a drink of champagne. "You left me out of the publication of the articles smuggled out of Spain last winter."

"And you ended up following me to the meeting in Hyde Park in any case. And though it was a good thing you did, or we'd have been hopelessly outnumbered when Lady Shroppington's agents attacked us, I do admit it probably would have been best if I'd confided in you from the start."

"Perhaps not for my relationship with my son. Which I appreciate your protecting."

Kitty smiled, quite as if they were discussing the antics of their younger children and not his relationship with his fellow-agent son who happened to be her former lover. "This doesn't threaten my relationship with anyone."

His gaze stayed intent but at the same time had a piercing

softness. "I was just telling Sofia it takes time to build a marriage. You and Julien deserve that time as well."

"What I do in Spain won't disturb Julien."

"Of course not. But Julien's in Parliament now. He may not be elected, but if he breaks the law, that can impact his ability to achieve change through legal channels."

"And you're now an advocate of change through legal channels?"

"I'm an advocate of change through as many channels as we can muster."

Kitty took a sip of champagne, keeping her gaze on his face. "I'm not Julien. My husband and I both know we'll have secrets from each other. Don't pretend you don't have secrets from Laura."

"I most certainly do. But I prefer not to put a friend in that situation."

Odd, there was a time she wouldn't have called Raoul a friend. But then, she wouldn't have called anyone a friend in those days. "Being friends has its complications."

"And its advantages."

Kitty unfurled her fan. "I told Julien from the start I wasn't going to lose who I am."

"Being married and being an agent is a juggling act, Kitty. I'm still learning how to juggle."

She wielded the fan, stirring air warm and heavy with close-pressed bodies, French scent, and hothouse roses. "Oh, so am I. But perhaps I have a head start. Juggling is almost a prerequisite for mothers."

"And fathers, if they're worthy of the name. Which many aren't."

"I'll grant that. Julien has a surprising knack for it. So do you."

"I'm trying." Raoul glanced down the passage. "Do you know if Cordelia and Mélanie and Laura got the papers?"

"No. I was actually looking for you because of that. Apparently, someone else took them off Dalton first."

"Well, that's an unforeseen complication."

"Did you see Dalton interact with anyone?" Kitty asked him.

"No." He frowned. "I used to be more alert."

"Not unusual for one mission to interfere with another."

"Not being able to balance two missions can get one killed in some situations. We're all going to need all our wits about us for the remainder of the night."

EMILY COWPER SLID her hand through Malcolm's arm. "Attempting to convert Trenchard?"

"Trying to nudge him to the left."

"Keep it up. I'm still working on my Harry. I have high hopes, eventually."

"Ah yes, but you have far greater influence over Palmerston than I could ever hope to with Trenchard."

Emily laughed. "Not the same sort, perhaps. But Trenchard respects your opinions. Of course, I rather think Harry respects mine. If I can change him, that will be why. He's too sensible to change his mind just because a woman bewitched him."

"I haven't doubted your talents since you were five years old, Em."

Emily laughed. "I do my best. I think the new Lord Carfax will be a good influence on Harry. And Harry likes Lady Carfax. I shall be charitable and say she may be a good influence, too. It's much easier to be charitable now I see how madly in love she is with her husband." She frowned a moment. "Odd to think of being in love with one's husband. I'm glad it works for some people."

Emily seemed very content in her marriage to Peter Cowper, an amiable union that allowed both partners to go their own way without worrying about fidelity. For that matter, Emily didn't seem too concerned with fidelity to Palmerston, her most serious lover, and the father, Malcolm was quite sure, of at least two of her children. Yet he didn't think he'd imagined the touch of wistfulness in her voice.

"There are different sorts of happiness, Em," he said.

"Goodness, yes. Life would be too dull, otherwise."

Emily was claimed by Granville Leveson-Gower for a dance, and Malcolm moved on. A piercing, unmistakable voice stopped him. "Rannoch."

"Lady Shroppington." It was not the first time Malcolm had faced a murderer who had escaped anything approaching justice, but it was the first he had done so in a friend's home. Well, unless one counted the former Lord Carfax.

Lady Shroppington raised a brow. "I expect you're surprised to see me here."

"On the contrary. After our interactions last winter, there's very little I'd be surprised to see you dare, ma'am."

"Humph." Lady Shroppington cast a glance round the ball-room. Couples were forming for a new waltz. "I confess, like the rest of the beau monde, I was curious to see what they made of the place. I feel badly for Amelia." Her gaze settled on the former Lady Carfax, who was talking with Lady Sefton. "She always had impeccable taste and instincts. She belonged here in a way Pamela Carfax never could."

"I'm sure I don't know what you mean." Malcolm felt his fingers tighten round his champagne glass.

"Don't be cheeky with me, Rannoch. Outsiders to the beau monde always have trouble. And obviously one can't expect them to ever really grasp what it means to belong. Given his background, one would think the new Lord Carfax might have chosen a more suitable bride."

That was brazen, considering Lady Shroppington had tried

to have Kitty killed. "His friends think he made a very suitable choice."

Lady Shroppington studied Kitty, who was speaking with Wellington and the Castlereaghs. Wellington was laughing and leaning close to her, and even the usually chilly Castlereaghs appeared to be smiling. "I admit she seems to know how to entertain. I expect your wife and Cordelia helped her."

"Kitty needs very little help in anything."

"It's an art running a place like Carfax House. And she wasn't born to it. She's doing better than I'd have expected. All this display seems rather a waste, though, if he's going to throw his prospects away with ridiculous causes."

"Ridiculous being in the eye of the beholder." Malcolm took a drink of champagne before he could succumb to impulse and break the glass in two. "I can think of a number of causes I'd call ridiculous. None of which the present Lord Carfax has been associated with. I can understand your disappointment, though. Given that you tried to recruit him yourself."

Lady Shroppington swung her gaze to him. It was steady but had gone as cold as her glittering diamond earrings. "I'm sure I don't know what you're talking about."

"Really, Lady Shroppington. Surely at this point we can take the gloves off."

"I don't care for boxing cant. I wouldn't have thought you'd be so vulgar."

"I can be a great many things, when pressed."

"You can't imagine I would let myself be drawn into a ridiculous conversation, here of all places."

"I don't see why not. It's true Jeremy Roth is here, but you've already proved yourself above the law."

Lady Shroppington's brows rose. "The Carfaxes invited a Bow Street runner?"

She sounded more aghast at what she saw as a social solecism than afraid of the man who had investigated the murder she'd been behind. Which was probably true.

"They've become good friends. The Carfaxes have a wide social circle."

"So it appears. If—"

"Lady Shroppington." Julien strolled up beside them, managing to emerge from the crowd so smoothly that even Malcolm didn't notice him in advance. "I'm glad you could join us."

Lady Shroppington couldn't quite control her start of surprise, but she kept her voice steady. "Very few would refuse an invitation to Carfax House on its reopening."

"It was hardly closed. It's been in the family all along."

"Am I to take it you consider yourself allied with your uncle? I thought you'd struck quite a different course."

"I don't think either Uncle Hubert or I has illusions we'll be allies in all things. But we have a healthy respect for each other. At least, I do for Uncle Hubert. You'd have to ask him what he thinks of me. And we share certain enemies. Neither of us is one to forget an enemy," Julien added with an easy smile. Malcolm could imagine him smiling in just that way as he stuck a knife in someone.

"Nor am I, Lord Carfax," said Lady Shroppington. Malcolm could imagine her smiling in that way as she dispatched an enemy as well.

"Lady Shroppington." Kitty, who had left Wellington and the Castlereaghs to make a circuit of the room, stopped beside them and slid her hand through the crook of Julien's arm. "It's good of you to join us." Her smile was as dazzling as plate armor.

"You've done an admirable job with the house, Lady Carfax. I'm sure invitations to your parties will be much sought after."

"You're too kind, ma'am. I doubt it, once the novelty wears off."

"Somehow, I imagine you and Lord Carfax will always be magnets of attention. Some people have a knack for it."

"It can be useful, at times," Julien said. "Whereas at other times, it's more useful to go quite unnoticed. As I'm sure you appreciate. I remember you from childhood, you know, Lady Shroppington. I remember your stopping to speak with my mother when we drove in Hyde Park. I remember just how you looked at her. And just what she thought of you."

"You're your mother's son. But you're still a Mallinson."

15

"*L*ady Shroppington." Cordelia had seen the other woman speaking with Malcolm, and then Julien and Kitty, and had watched Lady Shroppington cross the ballroom in her own direction. She'd known speech was inevitable, but words still failed her. What on earth did one say to a murderer when she was also one of one's grandmother's oldest friends? And when one was meeting in another friend's ballroom? It would have been very satisfying to give Lady Shroppington the cut direct, but it wouldn't be fair to Julien and Kitty to create a scene. Or, more important, to go against Julien's desire to use the ball to learn everything they could about Lady Shroppington and her surprising connection to the Elsinore League.

"Cordelia." Lady Shroppington greeted her in precisely the same manner she had before Cordelia had learned she had ordered Lewis Thornsby's murder. But then, Cordelia wouldn't have expected any less of her. Lady Shroppington ran a gaze over Cordelia, as though judging whether her gown was cut too low. And very likely also appraising how much she knew about the events of last January.

Cordelia summoned up a sweet smile designed to imply that she perhaps knew less than the full truth. After all, if she did, surely she wouldn't be able to be civil. And Lady Shroppington, for all her own abilities, was likely to underestimate Cordelia's abilities and the degree to which the Rannochs and Harry and the others took her into their confidence.

"It's quite splendid, isn't it?' Cordelia waved her fan to take in the ballroom and let her eyes open wide. "I told Kitty to make the most of it. One only has one chance to make a first impression. All Mayfair have been talking about them for weeks."

"Which can be a mixed blessing. In my day, we didn't revel in scandal."

"Dear ma'am. I thought in your day you were much franker about your scandals than we are. We tend to make much too much of a fuss."

"Perhaps. Though your own behavior would have been a scandal in any era. Whatever we did in my day, we didn't actually run off with men who weren't our husbands. And this matter of lost heirs emerging from the woodwork seems more suited to the pages of fiction than to Debrett's. Too much of it and people will start doubting settled inheritance."

"Oh dear, do you think it's a Radical plot?" Cordelia kept her eyes wide, though she wondered if she was skirting too close to the events of last January.

Lady Shroppington's gaze narrowed. "Given the path the new Lord Carfax has set out on, it wouldn't surprise me. But not with Carfax—Hubert Mallinson—involved."

"In any case, one can hardly blame the new Lord Carfax for the circumstances of his disappearance and reemergence."

"That depends on if we've had the full story. I'm not at all sure we have." Lady Shroppington's gaze swept the ballroom, which seemed to be growing more crowded by the minute. "It's an eclectic crowd, to say the least."

"Lord and Lady Carfax have a number of friends from various parts of their lives."

"So it would seem." She frowned across the ballroom at a couple waltzing on the edge of the dance floor. "Is that Sandy Trenor?"

The Elsinore League had shown an interest in Sandy, possibly because he was Alistair Rannoch's son, despite publicly being claimed by his mother's husband. Wariness shot over Cordelia; at the same time, she knew this was a good opportunity to gather information. "Yes, he's friends with the Rannochs, and now with the Carfaxes."

"And that young woman he's dancing with—is she—?"

"That's Miss Simcox."

"I don't know the name." Lady Shroppington's gaze widened, then hardened. "Oh, lord. She's the trollop he's taken up with, isn't she?"

"Miss Simcox is a friend of mine." There were limits to how far Cordelia was prepared to dissimulate to draw Lady Shroppington out.

"You're too free in your friendships, Cordelia. Especially for a woman with your past. You haven't swept everything under the rug, you know. Scandal can always catch hold again at the smallest spark. And you have two daughters to think of."

"I think about Livia and Drusilla a great deal. Among other things, I want to show them the value of standing by a friend."

"You're starting to talk the sort of democratic twaddle Rannoch spouts off. You, at least, know how the game is played."

Cordelia unfurled her fan. "I spent far too much time playing society's games. And they didn't serve me well in the end."

"That's because you broke the rules." Lady Shroppington's gaze was hard, but not unkind.

"And in doing so, I learned who my true friends are."

Lady Shroppington's gaze returned to Sandy. "One would

think someone would have brought that boy to his senses. I suppose the Rannochs are encouraging this folly. It's all very well for him to keep a mistress, but what possessed the Carfaxes to invite her?"

"Lady Shroppington, you can't believe she's the only mistress present."

"Don't play word games with me, Cordelia. You know there's a world of difference between a lady who indulges in such behavior—even one who does so as flagrantly as you did—and a girl of that type."

"There's a difference in how society treats them."

"Precisely. I hope you've learned discretion, if you're ever tempted to stray again."

"If I ever strayed again, I rather think I'd have a conversation with Harry and do it openly, and I hope he'd do the same. But I don't expect that to happen. With either of us."

To her surprise, Lady Shroppington laughed. "You think you can shock me. But the truth is my generation were far more ruthless than yours. We simply got on with what we did without imbuing it with so many emotions. And we took care to preserve the society about us. Which allowed us the freedom to do as we pleased."

"I quite agree you were more ruthless." Cordelia took a sip of champagne to soften her words in case she had let her mask slip too much.

"And we never made the mistake of confusing marriage and love." Lady Shroppington downed the last of her own champagne. "If you hadn't done so, you'd have been more content in your marriage to begin with."

"If I hadn't realized I loved Harry, I wouldn't have gone back to him."

Lady Shroppington frowned. Oddly, she looked concerned, more like the grandmother's friend Cordelia remembered from the long-ago days before her own scandal, and certainly before she'd known Lady Shroppington was a murderer. "Love is a poor foundation for a marriage, Cordelia. I worry about what will happen to you when this newfound love fades."

"I don't expect it to do so. More remarkably, I don't think Harry's will, either."

"That's because your generation are impossibly romantic. I can't think what brought it about. It wasn't Lord Byron, whatever people say. He merely made money off something that was already entrenched long before. Inside or outside a marriage, love never does last. That's why, while it may be the basis for a love affair, it's nothing to build a marriage on. I told Rannoch he might feel differently about his wife's theatrical adventures when he wasn't so besotted. And the current Carfax may regret marrying a Spanish adventuress when he's not quite so dazzled as he obviously is just now."

"The former Lord Carfax still seems quite fond of his wife," Cordelia couldn't resist saying.

Lady Shroppington frowned. "He and Amelia have always seemed fonder than most. But mark my words, both of them know it's not what marriage is built on. And I'm not sure they're as fond now as they used to be. You wouldn't know anything about that, would you?"

Presumably, with her connections to the League, Lady Shroppington knew about Gisèle, though there was no way to be sure. "Dear ma'am. You can hardly imagine Harry or I, of all people, have a great deal of knowledge of the Carfaxes' domestic arrangements."

"No, I suppose not." Lady Shroppington peered at Cordelia, who had the oddest feeling her mask was being tugged to see how securely it fit.

Cordelia resisted the urge to look away when out of the corner of her eye she saw George Dalton lurching through the crowd, face less flushed than it had been, hair disordered, gaze unfocused but also bright with rage. "Forgive me, Lady Shroppington. I believe Sir George is looking for me, and I must speak with him." She hurried towards him before Lady Shroppington could reply. "Oh, Sir George, there you are." Cordelia swept up to him and put a hand on his arm. "Are you feeling better?" she asked in a lowered tone. "I was a bit concerned, but thought it was best to let you sleep."

"You." Sir George gripped her other arm. "What have you done?"

"Oh, I just went back into the ballroom. You know the sort of talk there would be if I disappeared into an antechamber with a gentleman for too long. Harry is the most tolerant of husbands, but I really can't abuse his trust, and, given the past, you must see that I have to be particularly careful."

"You took them—"

"I assure you I didn't take anything. Pray don't be embarrassed, Sir George. I've seen many gentlemen in such a condition."

"By God, Lady Cordelia, I will not be trifled with."

"I should hope you wouldn't accuse me of trifling with you. Do watch your language, Sir George. Lady Shroppington is right behind me." Which was interesting, in that Lady Shroppington had likely tasked him with selling the papers, but of course neither of them could admit to it.

Sir George's shoulders straightened. He might well not want Lady Shroppington to know he had failed.

"Do let's go where we can discuss this in private," Cordelia said. She turned round. "Lady Shroppington, will you excuse us?"

Lady Shroppington was making a show of hanging back, but Cordelia suspected she had overheard a great deal. "Is this gentleman bothering you, Cordelia? Are you in need of assistance?"

"Oh, no, I assure you, ma'am. Just something Sir George and I need to discuss."

"Cordelia." Lady Shroppington caught her arm in a strong grip. "You had much better not be seen to leave the room alone with a gentleman given your reputation."

"Dear ma'am." Cordelia wrenched her arm from Lady Shroppington's grip. "My reputation is already in tatters."

"Lady Shroppington." Lady Frances was suddenly in front of them. "I've been looking everywhere for you. The Duke of York desires to speak with you."

Checkmate. Cordelia took Sir George's arm and dragged him through the crowd into an embrasure. He dropped down on a bench, still not quite steady on his feet, and pushed his disordered hair out of his eyes. "Don't come the innocent with me. You took the papers. Slipped something in my drink too, or someone did. Never should have risked dancing with one of the Rannoch crowd."

"No, you shouldn't." Cordelia sat beside him. "But the papers had already been replaced with dummies before we searched you."

He blinked. She wasn't sure if he was more shocked at this news or at the fact that she'd admitted it.

"So the question would seem to be who took them." Cordelia pressed up her advantage.

"You did. You're just making that up."

"In which case, why would I waste time with you?"

His brows drew together over his still slightly unfocused eyes.

"Look at it this way," Cordelia said. "If we'd got the papers, we'd have burned them long since. So if I'm lying, there's nothing you can do. But if I'm telling the truth, there may be a chance to recover the papers." Not that she was going to let him get his hands on them.

His frowned deepened.

"Only you can figure out who might have got hold of them," Cordelia said. "Who might have taken them from you?"

"Blaming me for this?"

"Well, obviously you lost them." Cordelia drew a breath. "That is, we need your expertise to solve this, Sir George."

He blinked again.

16

"My compliments." Carfax—Hubert—fell into place beside Malcolm in the yellow salon. "You managed it very adroitly."

"Managed what?" Malcolm smiled at his former spymaster. He had just asked Addison to question the footmen. Now he could probably help most by distracting Hubert.

"Let's not play games, Malcolm. I don't know which of you actually did it, but it's evidently one of your group. I think we're after the same thing tonight."

Malcolm met Hubert's gaze. "I don't know what you're talking about."

"I said let's not play games. I assume you have the letters? I hope we can negotiate."

"We don't have them."

"Very funny."

"It's not funny at all." Malcolm braced a hand against the gilded molding. "Someone else got to them before we did. Any idea who that might be?"

Hubert's brows drew together. "That's a terrible story. No one of sense would believe it for a moment."

"Quite."

"So if you're trying it—"

"It either has to be a complicated gambit or the truth. Your choice."

The frown deepened. "Who the devil—"

"Your guess is as good as mine. Most of the people here tonight would like those letters."

Hubert grimaced. "Brougham's going to be a nuisance for the next six months, at least."

"Brougham's a showman, but he has sincere beliefs."

"Yes, that's the problem." Hubert pushed up his spectacles. "Brougham wouldn't cavil at using a lady's personal correspondence for his own ends. So I'd actually think you'd prefer I got them. I obviously won't make them public."

"Not for the same reason Brougham would. But if you found something in them that would be useful to the king's cause, you can't tell me you wouldn't use it."

"I'd—"

"Otherwise, you wouldn't mind my retrieving the letters and burning them."

Hubert adjusted his right earpiece. "Surely even you see the disaster that could ensue if the king became too unpopular."

"Such as the country's ceasing to believe in hereditary monarchy?"

Hubert gave a wry grimace as he adjusted the left earpiece. "All right. It was worth a try."

"You're usually more adroit. For what it's worth, I don't think the king will topple. But I also think the queen is being ill used."

"If it were just a matter of the two of them, I'd cheerfully leave them to sort it out for themselves. But of course, it isn't."

"Rather making the argument against hereditary monarchy." Malcolm folded his arms. "I don't suppose you've gained any insights from your friends in the Elsinore League?"

"They're hardly friends."

"With you, the word 'friend' is a bit elastic."

"They're too clever to reveal anything."

"Dalton was fool enough to lose the letters."

"Dalton's just an agent."

"An agent they trusted with a commission he bungled."

Hubert grimaced. "Yes, that was sloppy work. But tell me you've never had an agent let you down."

"I've even been known to let my superiors down, as I recall. Though I don't think I've ever been this sloppy."

"Don't fish for compliments, Malcolm. You know perfectly well you haven't."

"All of which dances round my original question. You've been determined to bring down the League for more than two decades. They've been openly at war with you for at least two years. And yet you're making deals with them."

"I wanted the papers. The League were willing to work with the highest bidder."

"You didn't wonder if they were setting you up?"

"Of course I did. I'd be extremely careful before I used the papers. But since my main objective was to keep them out of Brougham's hands, it made sense to buy them."

"We're supposed to be allies against the League, at the moment."

"And we are. But being allies in one thing doesn't make us allies in everything." Hubert tugged at his shirt cuff. "I should have thought your wife and father would have taught you that."

SANDY HELD out his arm to Bet. "You're smiling."

Bet felt her smile deepen as she took his arm. "I'm glad we came. It's good to be reminded of how many friends we have."

He grinned, and for a moment it was as though they were at

home instead of in the midst of a vast ballroom where half the guests probably wouldn't acknowledge her if they knew who she was. "I think I'm done doing my duty," Sandy said. "Mama and Father don't seem to have come after all. We can have supper together. With Lucan and Nan. I'll scout out a good table—"

He broke off, his gaze locked on a tall dark-haired woman in midnight blue satin and sapphires. Bet had only seen her from a distance, but she recognized Sandy's mother at once. She pulled her hand from Sandy's arm and stepped back, but Sandy caught her hand. "Mama." Sandy inclined his head.

"Alexander." Lady Marchmain took a step forwards, gaze on Sandy. In fact, Bet suddenly knew what it was like to be treated as though one were invisible. "Come with me. There's someone I want to present you to."

Bet did her best to melt into the background, but Sandy's grip on her hand tightened with determination. He'd always been careful to keep her away from his parents, but apparently it was a different thing when they were all actually thrown together. "I can't now, Mama. We're just on our way in to supper. I don't believe you met Miss Simcox."

Lady Marchmain's eyes widened in horror. "I don't know what's worse. That you brought her here or that you have the effrontery to attempt to introduce me to your common—"

"Mama," Sandy said, in a voice like ice. "Don't say anything neither of us will be able to get past."

Lord Marchmain stepped up beside his wife. He had graying blond hair and a tired face, but his eyes, Bet thought, were not unkind. As he put a hand on his wife's arm, Bet felt a flash of unexpected solidarity. They were both trying to prevent a scene. "No need for a disturbance, Helen. It's a pleasure to meet you at last, Miss Simcox. We've heard a great deal about you."

"Thank you." Bet curtsied and managed to keep her voice steady.

Spots of crimson darker than her rouge showed on Lady Marchmain's cheeks. "Marcus—"

"We must let Sandy escort Miss Simcox into supper, Helen. I wouldn't have it be said he was derelict in his duty."

Sandy held his arm out to Bet. Bet took it—this seemed the safest way out of the conversation for all of them.

"I'm sorry," Sandy murmured, white-lipped, as they went through the archway to the supper room. "I should never have exposed you to that."

"I shouldn't have come," Bet said, keeping her voice matter-of-fact. "It was bound to be awkward for all of us."

"It wouldn't have been awkward at all if Mama could have been civil or at least kept her distance if she couldn't manage civility. She's disappointed me a great deal lately. But I didn't think she'd stoop—"

"Sandy." Bet tightened her fingers on his arm. "She's your mother. No matter what. Family are important. Don't ever let anything come before that."

Sandy looked down at her, his features tight, then seemed to force a smile to his face. "Let's enjoy supper. There are Lucan and Nan. I told them to find a table."

Sam and Nan were at a table on the edge of the room, thank goodness. Sam was leaning over to speak with a gentleman at the next table. Rupert Caruthers, Bet realized. He was a viscount and an MP but he was a friend of the Rannochs' and now of hers as well. Nan waved to them.

"Good to meet an old friend," Sam said as Sandy and Bet joined them.

"Lucan was my best supplier in the Peninsula when I needed things unofficially," Rupert said with an easy smile. "And yes, I knew even then he supplied the opposite side as well. More often, I think."

"I did have my preferences," Sam said. "No offense."

"None taken."

Bertrand Laclos joined them. "Lucan supplied me, too. When I was undercover working with the French." He dropped into a chair beside Rupert with an easy smile. Bertrand had been a formidable agent, and now, though no one had ever quite said as much to Bet, she knew he helped former Bonapartists escape the Continent. And she also knew, though no one had ever quite put it into words either, that he and Rupert were lovers. "I flattered myself Lucan didn't know I was a double," Bertrand added.

"Oh, I was taken in all right," Sam said. "Half the time I couldn't even recognize you in your different disguises. But then, there were plenty who worked for different sides. Including our host. Still can't get over the idea of him as someone—"

"Safe?" Nan asked.

"Someone who believes in something."

"Yes," Bertrand said. "He has a lot of surprises. I met him once or twice on missions. Under different identities."

"But you could recognize him?" Bet asked.

"Yes." Bertrand smiled. "At least, there were times I recognized him. Not at once. And I wouldn't be at all surprised if there were other times I encountered him and still don't know whom I was dealing with."

"Sam says Lady Carfax was just as formidable." Nan said.

"She was," Rupert said. "They both still are."

Sam shot a look at him. "We're on a battlefield right now, aren't we?"

"Perhaps a tilting field would be more accurate," Rupert said. "But tonight is definitely a shot across the bow, if I'm not mixing my metaphors."

They got plates of food and somehow Rupert and Bertrand turned their chairs round to join the table Bet and Sandy were sharing with Nan and Sam, and Bet found she was laughing and not worrying about Sam and Nan and almost forgot about Sandy's parents for seconds at a time. She was giggling at a joke Rupert had made when a scream sounded from the table on the other side.

"My bracelet! It's gone!"

*B*et looked up to see a stout lady in a puce satin turban and gown clutching her wrist.

"Must have fallen off," said a red-faced gentleman seated beside her.

"Don't you think I'd have realized?" she said.

"You don't know what's happening with your jewels half the time. You'd lose your head if it wasn't attached to your neck."

Rupert pushed his chair back and got to his feet. "I'm sure it's somewhere about, Lady Derby. Let us help you look."

Bertrand and Sandy got up to join in the search as well, and after they did, Bet, Nan, and Sam also did, holding back a bit, as none of them knew the Derbys. Others from nearby tables joined in as well. A flurry of search followed, including some indecorous poking under Lady Derby's skirts. "I tell you it couldn't have fallen off," Lady Derby said. "I just had the stones cleaned and reset, and Rundle & Bridge checked the clasp." She scanned the group now clustered round her table. "You." Her gaze fastened on Sam.

"I beg pardon, ma'am?" Sam straightened up. He was on his

knees, looking under the table with the aid of a candle taken from their own table.

Lady Derby stared down at him as though he were a rat that had crawled out from beneath the damask tablecloth. "You stole it."

"I what?" Sam sat back on his heels. "No, upon my word. Wouldn't dream of such a thing, ma'am. I'm sure the bracelet is about here somewhere."

"You would say that. You jostled up against me at the buffet table."

Sam's shoulders straightened. "Madam, I did not—"

"Lady Derby." Sandy pushed himself to his feet on the other side of the table. "There must be some mistake. Mr. Lucan is a friend of mine."

"He's a friend of all of ours," Rupert said, getting to his feet as well.

"Who is Mr. Lucan?" Lady Derby demanded.

"The gentleman you've accused," Bertrand said. "We were all sharing supper a few moments before. Upon my honor, he would never do anything of the sort."

"It's not your honor I'm concerned with, Mr. Laclos. It's his."

"Mr. Lucan's honor is unimpeachable," Sandy said.

"Good of you, Trenor, but no need to make a fuss." Sam blew out the candle.

"I'm afraid you're not to be trusted, Alexander," Lady Derby said. "Everyone knows the company you consort with these days."

Sandy's gaze grew cold in a way Bet had never seen. "What precisely are you referring to, Lady Derby?"

"I think it's plain enough." Lady Derby's gaze shot to Bet, who had gone still kneeling beside Sandy.

"Do not force me to take offense, Lady Derby," Sandy said.

"Sandy—" Bet pushed herself to her feet and plucked at his sleeve.

"Lady Derby," Rupert said, before Sandy could speak, "perhaps we could repair to one of the salons—"

"With my bracelet in this room? I think not."

"The footmen can organize a search," Bertrand said.

"There's no need to search," Lady Derby declared.

"Lady Derby—" Sandy said in a voice that sent a chill of fear through Bet.

"I appreciate it, Trenor, but let me handle this." Sam took a step round the table towards Lady Derby. "I don't have the bracelet, madam. I'm not a thief. And if you don't believe that, believe that I'd be a fool to have taken it under these circumstances."

"Why should I believe anything you say?" Lady Derby asked.

Sandy drew a breath of outrage. "Because—"

"I demand we send to Bow Street," Lady Derby said, gaze on Sam.

"No need to send anywhere." Jeremy Roth emerged from the crowd. Bet breathed a sigh of relief. Not only was Jeremy Roth a Bow Street runner, he was eminently sensible. And as he was not one of the beau monde, either, she'd always felt a certain kinship with him. "Lady Derby, we can begin an investigation into the loss of your bracelet," Roth said. "Perhaps we could speak in one of the anterooms."

"I will not be moved into an anteroom, and there's no need to investigate. That man took it." Lady Derby gestured at Sam. "Search him."

"I can scarcely search a fellow guest."

"See here, my good man," Lord Derby said to Sam. "Empty out your pockets."

Roth turned to Sam. "You have no need to follow such a suggestion."

"On the contrary. Glad to do it." Sam drew himself up to his full height. He could have bested most of the men in the room. So could Nan. But his expression spoke of wounded pride, not an impulse to battle. He emptied out his pockets onto the damask tablecloth laden with plates and glasses with the dignity of a judge, while the crowd looked on with interest. Coins. A pocketknife. A small wooden horse that belonged to Nan's daughter Sarah. A perfume vial that was probably Nan's. A pack of cards. Two spare buttons. And then, just as he stared at them with the contempt of one who has proved his case, the unmistakable glitter of diamonds.

Sam stared at the sparkling stones and white gold in disbelief, momentarily robbed of speech. Bet heard Nan draw a sharp breath, then saw her clamp her lips shut.

Lady Derby snatched up the bracelet and held it aloft. "Proof. How dare you!" The stones caught the candlelight. "Arrest him." Her gaze shot to Roth.

"I'll do nothing of the sort. Lady Derby, you must realize that if Mr. Lucan had actually taken the bracelet, there'd have been no reason for him to agree to voluntarily empty out his pockets."

"What are you suggesting?" Lord Derby demanded. "That someone deliberately planted the bracelet on Lucan?"

"That seems to be the obvious conclusion."

"Why, in God's name?"

"Why indeed?"

"Must have been that girl." Lady Derby's gaze went to Bet. "She wanted it."

Sandy surged forwards, pulling free of Bet's grasp on his arm. "You will retract that remark, madam."

"Going to challenge Lady Derby to a duel, Sandy?" Someone in the crowd let out a rough laugh.

"I won't stand by while she commits slander."

"What seems to be the trouble?" Lord Carfax—Julien, as Bet was learning to call him because she couldn't call him "Mr. St. Juste" anymore—strolled through the crowd, which somehow parted without his doing any pushing. Bertrand was behind him. Only then did Bet realize that Bertrand had melted away from the crowd in that quiet way he could. He must have gone to fetch Julien.

Julien cast a look of inquiry round, though Bet was sure Bertrand had already briefed him on what was happening. He raised a brow in a way that seemed to dare everyone to ruffle the cool waters in the supper room.

"This man stole my bracelet," Lady Derby said. "Or that girl did and put it in his pocket."

Sandy's hands curled into fists. Julien dropped a hand on his shoulder, a fraction of a second, Bet thought, before Sandy lunged at Lady Derby. "I'm sure there's some misunderstanding. I'm quite sure my friends would do nothing of the sort."

"The bracelet was in his pocket," Lord Derby said.

"And he turned out his pockets without a blink," Roth said. "The bracelet appears to have been planted on Mr. Lucan without his knowledge."

"By—" Lady Derby began.

Julien held up a hand before Sandy could take umbrage again. "I fail to see what the fuss is about. You have your bracelet back, Lady Derby?"

"Yes. But—"

"They look like particularly fine stones." Lady Carfax—Kitty —slipped through the crowd to stand beside Julien. "I'm so glad you have it safely back, Lady Derby. It must be a great relief. I can quite see why you were concerned."

"Yes, but having it back doesn't explain how it disappeared. It didn't slip off my wrist into that man's pocket."

"No, indeed," Julien agreed in a cordial voice. "I can't know for a certainty, of course, but I would say this has all the hallmarks of an undergraduate prank. I never attended university myself, but I'm familiar enough with stories from friends to know the type of action."

"You think someone took my bracelet and put it in Mr. Lucan's pocket as a prank?" Lady Derby demanded.

"Why else would someone take a bracelet and hide it in the pocket of a quite unconnected person?"

Lady Derby opened her mouth as though to object, but apparently could not frame adequate words.

"All settled, I think," Julien said. "My apologies, Lucan. I'm sure when Lady Derby recovers the power of speech, she will tender her apologies for the inconvenience to you and to Miss Simcox, as well."

"No matter." Sam waved a hand. "I'm fine."

"So am I." Bet tucked her hand through Sandy's arm, willing him to restraint.

"You must all have some more champagne," Kitty said before anyone could protest. "Oh, good. Here's Giles with a fresh bottle just in time."

1 8

———

"***O***ut with it, Sylvie." Julien fell into step beside Sylvie St. Ives, fingers curled round her gloved arm before she even turned to look at him. "Why did you do it?"

"Why did I do what?"

Julien tightened his grip on her arm. "Plant Lady Derby's bracelet on Lucan."

Sylvie pulled free of his grip and smoothed her glove. "What on earth makes you think I did that?"

"Among other things, because you're one of the few people present with the skills to carry it off."

Sylvie pulled away from him and slid a gold bracelet up her arm. "Don't be silly, Julien. Either of the Rannochs or the O'Roarkes or the Davenports—probably all four of them— could have done it. Your wife certainly could have done it."

"Point taken. Which leaves aside the fact that none of them would have a motive."

"And I would? I have several lovely diamond bracelets. Lady Derby's is a vulgar setting and the stones are inferior."

"You seem well acquainted with it." Julien made no move to grip her arm again, but he positioned himself leaning against the wall where he could easily block her if she moved in any direction.

Sylvie adjusted the gold bandeau that matched her bracelet. "I was as intrigued by the fuss as everyone else in the supper room. If I'd taken the bracelet I'd have disappeared by now."

"Oh, no, you're much too clever to have done that."

"None of which explains why I'd have taken it."

"How better to create a diversion?"

Sylvie's eyes widened. "Why on earth would I have wanted to do that?"

"You tell me."

"Darling Julien. If I'd wanted to create a diversion, surely I'd have taken advantage of the commotion rather than remaining in the ballroom."

"Not if you were creating it for someone else. Are you still working for Fouché?"

"Don't waste time with rhetorical questions, Julien. Not that I particularly want to help you, but for old times' sake I'd advise you not to waste time with me at all. Your real culprit is getting away."

Julien folded his arms across his chest and regarded his former comrade and lover through narrowed eyes. Every so often Sylvie had a point.

Just possibly, this was one of those times.

"ANY LUCK?" Raoul stopped beside Mélanie on the edge of the ballroom floor.

"Not yet." Mélanie looked at her former spymaster. "I'm looking for Addison. Blanca said he was talking to the footmen. And Cordelia was talking to Dalton. I didn't want to interfere."

He gave a quick smile. "Always hard to wait."

"Ghastly."

"You missed all the fun." Kitty slipped through the crowd to join them.

"Did Dalton try anything else?" Mélanie asked. "I thought Cordy had him."

"Not Dalton. Someone planted Lady Derby's bracelet on Sam Lucan. Presumably to create a distraction. It's all right. Everything's smoothed over. But I'm wondering who wanted the distraction. And why. Julien thinks it was Sylvie. But I'm not so sure."

"Interesting," Raoul said.

"It's someone who wants the papers. Or—" Mélanie looked from Raoul to Kitty.

"Quite," Raoul said. "Obviously an attempt at distraction. But given that someone has the papers—"

"How much help would that really be?" Kitty said. "It wouldn't distract the person who'd taken the papers—"

"Mélanie. Kitty. Raoul." Nerezza Russo, who was the beloved of Lord Beverston's younger son Benedict, swept up to them. Her gaze was controlled, but she had an air of suppressed excitement. And yet she and Ben didn't know about the letters. At least, not as far as Mélanie knew.

"It's Lord Beverston," Nerezza said. "He slipped out of the ballroom about ten minutes ago. Ben and I followed him because it seemed odd. He didn't see us. We were careful. But we saw him go into Lord Carfax's—Julien's—study. We thought about confronting him. Well, Ben wanted to. But I pointed out that he had no authority here and his father would just defy him. So Ben's keeping watch near the study door, and I came to get you."

Kitty exchanged quick looks with Mélanie and Raoul. "Quite right. Thank you, Nerezza. It seems I need to have a word with Ben's father. Because I do have authority in this house."

∼

BENEDICT SMYTHE HAD CONCEALED himself in the shadows behind the long-case clock in the hall. Excellently done. Even Kitty didn't notice him at first, and yet if one did notice him, he wasn't obviously hiding.

"Well done." Kitty stopped beside him. "You're learning."

"Trying." Ben flashed her a brief, concerned smile. "Father hasn't come out."

"Good." Kitty squeezed his arm and swept up to the study where she had met with her former spymaster, the room that was now her husband's sanctum. She approached the door as silently as possible and flung it open abruptly.

Lord Beverston spun round. Something clattered to the Turkey rug. "Lady Carfax—I was just—"

"Going through my husband's things." Kitty swept forwards with the speed with which she would retrieve a dropped weapon in a fight and snatched up the fallen object. "And apparently taking"—she glanced down at the object in her hand—"a snuff box?"

Lord Beverston met her gaze, his blue eyes cool despite his earlier blunder. "It's a particularly fine one. I noticed it and had picked it up to look at the enamel when you surprised me by opening the door so suddenly."

"Into my husband's study." Kitty stared at Beverston standing beside Julien's desk. Hubert Mallinson's former desk. She and Julien had indulged in some activities more suited to the bedchamber than the study on that desk on one memorable evening. Part of making the room and the house their own.

"I came down here to leave a message for Carfax," Beverston said.

Kitty folded her arms, the snuff box securely closed in her fingers. "Do let's stop playing games, Lord Beverston. We both know perfectly well you came here to take something on Elsinore League business."

Beverston, to his credit, did not shy away from her gaze. "I think we both know one can't simply talk about Elsinore League business anymore, Lady Carfax."

"Very well. Business for your faction in the Elsinore League."

"Which makes us closer allies than you might think."

"Then do you want to tell me why you took this snuff box?"

"Surely you of all people realize allies don't—can't—share everything." Beverston's gaze was hard but level.

Kitty returned the gaze like the challenge it was. "Then surely you'll understand why I ask you to leave this room at once."

"Courage, *querida*," Raoul said. "There'll be something for you to do before too long."

Mélanie pulled a face at him. "I'm not that bad."

"I'll own to considerable frustration myself." Raoul leaned against a convenient column. "I'm just more used to it."

"I didn't see you for much of the night."

"I was making a circuit of the rooms," he said in an easy voice. "Trying to draw attention on the periphery. Especially since Laura had a more important role to play."

It made sense and Malcolm had been doing much the same. But something still did not ring quite right. She opened her mouth to question him, when Cordelia came hurrying up to them, dragging Addison. She was breathing quickly and one of her curls had escaped her bandeau.

"I startled Dalton into talking," Cordelia said. "I think he's telling the truth. I have a list of who he danced with. Also, someone jostled him and spilled port on his coat in the card-room earlier in the evening. We didn't know because it must have been when Archie wasn't in the room. Dalton couldn't see who jostled was. He went into the gentleman's retiring room to sponge off his coat, and he removed the coat to attend to a stain on his neckcloth. He says no one else was in the room. But if there are curtains someone could hide behind—"

"There are," Raoul said. "If he was distracted, that could serve. Does he remember who was nearby when he was jostled?"

"He wouldn't tell me. He may believe I don't have the letters, but he knows we have different agendas for recovering them. But Addison questioned the footmen." Cordelia turned to Addison.

"One of them was nearby when the incident occurred." Addison pulled a list from his shirt cuff. "He was hired on for tonight and didn't know the names of many of the guests, but I was able to put his description together with my knowledge of the guests and identify most of them." He glanced down at the list. "I believe Mr. Tarkington is a member of the Levellers."

"He is," Mélanie said, even as she heard Raoul draw in his breath. She looked at him.

"I suggest we talk to Sofia Montagu," Raoul said. "I didn't realize it at the time, but thinking back, I suspect she may have papers concealed in her bodice."

Mélanie watched her former spymaster for a moment. He didn't elaborate on how he knew. She didn't think he'd danced with Sofia tonight, though she might have missed it. Raoul returned her gaze levelly, with no hint that he'd explain later. Which was interesting, but not something to examine just now.

"I'll get Malcolm," she said. "If anyone can make Kit and Sofia see sense, he can."

~

"I believe you have something, Sofia," Mélanie said. "Something we desperately needed to retrieve but that is rightfully the property of Lady Wilton."

Sofia raised her brows in perfect surprise. Just as Mélanie would herself in the same circumstances. "I don't even know Lady Wilton."

"I make you my compliments," Mélanie said. "In many ways, your plan was cleverer than ours. And you got to Dalton first."

"You've lost me." Kit was almost as good at dissimulating as Sofia.

Malcolm braced his hands on the table behind him in the antechamber off the yellow salon. "We don't expect you to admit it. Neither of us would do so in the same circumstances. And it was crucial to get the papers away from the League and Carfax both. But you must see that we can't use them or give them to anyone who would." Malcolm looked from Kit to Sofia with a hard gaze. "We can't let anyone else see those letters, certainly not the general public."

"But the information—" Kit bit back his words just short of an admission.

"Could destroy a woman's life," Malcolm said.

"It could save Queen Caroline," Sofia said. She looked at Kit. "They know. There's no sense denying it."

"At the cost of damaging a woman who did nothing save confide things to a man whom she had fallen in love with," Malcolm said, "with no thought of being part of this public circus."

Uncertainty shot through Kit's gaze. He was no stranger to scandal, and he was usually keenly sensitive to a lady's reputation. But there was also a hardness beneath the uncertainty that hadn't been there when Mélanie first met him in Italy. And he was committed to the Levellers, a group of young Radicals dedicated to bringing about change. Much-needed change. Mélanie knew a great deal about how far the desire for change could push one.

"Malcolm," Kit said, in a voice somehow at once entreating and imploring, "you know what it could mean if the queen triumphs. If the king loses power, so do his allies. Who knows how it could shift the balance in Parliament. Imagine the bills that might pass. Repealing the corn laws and enclosure, Catholic Emancipation, abolition, your capital punishment bill—"

"My God, you think I don't imagine that?" Malcolm's voice cut with unexpected force.

"And?" Kit's gaze was like the flat of a sword blade.

"You're always saying you don't trust Parliament."

"And you're always saying one has to work within the system as well as outside it."

"This is your idea of working within the system?" Malcolm countered. "Ruining a woman's life?"

Kit flushed.

"It's not Lady Wilton's life that's the issue," Sofia said.

"No," Mélanie agreed. "Lady Wilton could become collateral damage. Because of private letters she wrote to a man she cared about."

"They're only letters—"

"They could destroy a marriage."

"Which is probably already damaged." Kit knew all about damaged marriages, having grown up in one.

"Perhaps," Malcolm said. "It's her choice if she wants to remain in it. My God, Kit, you know what it's like to grow up separated from one of your parents. And very few men would follow your father's lead and leave the children with their wife. She could lose her children."

"Like the queen lost Princes Charlotte," Sofia said. "I met the queen when she lived on Lake Como. She kept saying how fortunate my mother was to still see her children after she separated from my father."

"Ruining Alice Wilton's life won't right that wrong," Malcolm said.

Sofia spun away to look at Kit. After a long moment, they

both dragged their gazes back to Malcolm and Mélanie. "So we cover up secrets?" It was Sofia who spoke first.

"We return the papers to the person who should have them," Malcolm said.

Sofia put her hand to the bodice of her gown. "Did you always make this sort of judgment in intelligence?"

"No." Malcolm touched her arm. "And I live with regrets I hope to God you never have."

"JULIEN." Kitty caught her husband's arm as she came through the archway from the upstairs passage into the ballroom. "I just caught Beverston in your study."

Julien's brows drew together. "For once, Sylvie may have been telling the truth. What was he doing?"

"Trying to steal this, apparently." Kitty put the snuff box in her husband's hand.

Julien frowned down at it, rare surprise on his face.

"Is it your father's?" Kitty asked.

"No." Julien studied the delicate enamel. "It's my grandfather's. Far older than the Elsinore League. Hard to imagine what the devil the significance could be—" He looked at it a moment longer, then glanced at the door from the salons. "Time to puzzle over this later. There are Malcolm and Mélanie. and from the looks on their faces, they have the papers. At least one of tonight's missions is accomplished."

2 0

Cordelia stretched her arms over her head and took a sip of champagne. "Tonight was a triumph."

"On multiple levels." Mélanie curled her feet up under her in the armchair she was sharing with Malcolm and lifted her glass to Kitty and Julien. They had seemed relaxed all night, but if their experience was anything like her own, they were only just starting to actually feel so, now the guests were gone. Talking with friends after a party was always her favorite part of entertaining.

"It's certainly a night a number of people won't forget." Kitty lifted her glass to Mélanie in return and then smiled at the whole group gathered in the Carfax House library. All those involved in the search for Alice Wilton's letters were present, and David and Simon, who had been brought up to date. "Though I can't say we had anything to do with that."

"On the contrary." Lady Frances let her violet zephyr scarf slither down about her on the sofa where she sat with her husband Archie. "Even before the incident with Lady Derby's bracelet, it was clear the night would be much talked of."

"Well, that should keep a number of them out of our hair." Julien was refilling whisky and champagne glasses.

"Not perhaps as many as you'd like." Frances tilted her champagne glass as he filled it. "You're going to be an endless source of fascination to the beau monde."

"More fools them." Julien righted the champagne bottle just in time for the bubbles to rise to the rim of Frances's glass. "No, I take that back. Kitty would be an endless source of fascination to anyone."

David stretched his legs out in front of him in an uncharacteristically relaxed pose and looked up at his cousin. "You've made an art of making yourself fascinating to people your entire life."

"I don't know about art." Julien splashed more whisky into David's glass. "But it can be useful, at times. Just as blending into the woodwork can be useful."

"It was very agreeable to have a mission again," Blanca said. She looked at Addison, who was perched on the arm of her chair. "Don't deny it, Miles."

"I wouldn't dream of it," Addison said.

"Progress, *mi amor.*" Blanca reached for his hand.

Andrew was sitting on the settee beside Gisèle, quiet as he usually was when surrounded by a coterie of spies. "Do you think the League will know Gelly warned you?"

"Given that Sofia and Kit and Brougham all knew about the letters, I doubt it," Malcolm said. "The news was obviously out."

Gisèle nodded. "I was careful. I know not to give you information that would blow my cover."

Malcolm regarded his sister for a long moment. Mélanie could feel her husband's concern. As much as they were now allies, there was a great deal about her relationship with the League—or rather, the faction in the League trying to take over —that she hadn't shared with him.

"How did Kit and Sofia learn about the letters?" Laura asked.

"Sofia's brother wrote to her," Mélanie said. "She says he got word from some of his Carbonari contacts. I'm still not sure we have the full story of how they discovered all of it. But then, even though they're allies and friends, we can't expect them to share everything, just as we don't share everything with them."

"Quite," Raoul said.

Mélanie looked at him for a moment, wondering yet again how he had determined Sofia had the letters. But then, it was understood that they didn't share everything with their own family, either. And it was like Raoul to confront that head-on.

"And that whole business with Lady Derby's bracelet had nothing to do with the letters, in the end?" Cordelia said.

"Apparently not." Julien paused beside the fireplace, champagne bottle in one hand, whisky decanter in the other. "Beverston seems to have set it up. To create a distraction so he could go into my study. Where his goal seems to have been to take my grandfather's snuff box. I confess to being at a loss as to why, at present."

"I found him taking the snuff box," Kitty said. "He could have been after more."

"True," Julien agreed. "But the snuff box obviously has some significance."

"Your grandfather died before the League was founded," Frances said.

"Yes." Julien moved to refill Malcolm's glass. "The snuff box would have gone to my father. It's a bit small to contain a hidden code or any sort of message. I shall certainly examine it, though."

"There's one other thing I don't understand," Edith said. "Was it just coincidence that Lewis Thornsby—befriended Alice Wilton? Or did the League set it up? Because it seems a lot of work, even for the League, to have set up their affair only to sell her letters to the highest bidder."

"I was thinking the same thing," Laura said.

"Quite." Malcolm turned his refilled whisky glass in his hand. "The League seem to be up to something complicated in Italy, probably involving Princess Caroline—the queen. And I very much doubt we've heard the last of it."

Julien set down the decanter and bottle and picked up his own glass. "Here's to the autumn."

MÉLANIE CLOSED the door of the night nursery, where their son Colin and daughter Jessica and Laura and Raoul's daughter Emily were sleeping. Colin had woken for a moment and asked about the ball when she went in to check on them, but now he too was back asleep. "I knew tonight would be challenging, and we'd all need our wits about us," she said to Malcolm. "But I had no notion quite how much."

"No. Though you'd think we'd be prepared for League intrigue at any moment." Malcolm was sitting on the edge of the bed, petting their cat, Berowne.

"And I think we're going to have to be prepared for intrigue round the queen and king at every turn in the coming months, as well." Mélanie sat beside him and ran her fingers over Berowne's soft gray head. "But I think we came though tonight quite well. And Julien and Kitty did splendidly."

Malcolm scratched Berowne under the chin. "I don't envy them the attention they're going to get from the beau monde. I'm glad to be out of it."

"We're not going to be able to stay out of it, darling. Not with the queen's trial engulfing political London. A lot of the fight's going to play out in drawing rooms and ballrooms."

"Once more unto the breach." Malcolm leaned back on his hands. The light from the candle on the night table caught the shadows round his eyes. "Even before the incident with Lady

Derby's bracelet, Sandy was struggling, balancing Bet's being there with his parents."

"Yes." Mélanie thought of the way Bet's gaze fastened on Sandy in unguarded moments. There had been one such moment tonight, when Sandy turned to a footman to get Bet a glass of champagne. Bet had been laughing, but for an instant she'd looked at Sandy as though committing every detail to memory. Mélanie had once looked at Malcolm that way, she suspected. She'd certainly lain awake trying to memorize the contours of his face against a moment when she might never see him again.

"I wish Bet weren't so generally known," Malcolm said. "That there was a way to devise a history for her, as we did for Rachel."

"That wouldn't really solve things, darling."

Malcolm rubbed Berowne between his ears. "It would if enough people believed it."

"Covering up her past wouldn't change the fact that prejudices are unjust."

He looked up into her eyes. "Well, no. It doesn't mean we should stop trying to change things. But meanwhile, it would make Sandy and Bet happy."

"You think he'd marry her if his parents wouldn't be scandalized?"

"Don't you?"

Mélanie pulled the pins from her hair and shook it our about her shoulders. "Not everyone is you, Malcolm."

"Oh, Sandy's much more sensible than I was at his age. He isn't afraid to admit what he wants."

"And he doesn't worry he doesn't deserve it."

Malcolm smiled. "That, too."

"But he doesn't have your flexibility of thinking."

"Can you look at him and doubt he's a man in love?"

"Love and marriage don't go hand in hand for a lot of people."

Malcolm's gaze settled on her own. "Sadly true." He leaned forwards across Berowne and put his mouth to hers. "How fortunate that we aren't among their number."

Julien pulled the stickpin from his cravat and regarded it. "Have I told you I'm proud of you, Kitkat?"

Kitty unclasped her necklace. "I had a lot of help from Mélanie and Cordy. And the servants did most of the work. As for the search for the papers, all the others got to do more than I did."

Julien set the stickpin beside his shaving kit. "Not the ball or the investigation, though both were a triumph. The way you fight for what you believe in."

Kitty laughed as she snapped her jewel box closed. "I'm a hardheaded pragmatist, my love."

"You're an idealist who can be ruthlessly practical about achieving your goals. Your ability to believe astonishes me. It's even kindled some embers in me."

Kitty turned, leaning against the dressing table, and studied her husband. "You've always believed in a lot, Julien. You just wouldn't admit to it."

Julien unwound his cravat. "I couldn't or wouldn't believe I could make a difference. Which perhaps was a way of letting myself off the hook. Staying out of the mess doesn't accomplish anything but let the bastards win."

She gave a rough laugh. "It's true I don't avoid messes. I've never been satisfied with what I find about me."

"Nor have I." Julien tossed the cravat in the laundry basket. "But I wasn't as focused as you. To put it mildly."

"It doesn't always make it easy for our family."

"It's going to make a better world for our children, I profoundly hope." Julien unfastened a shirt cuff but paused, the button held between two fingers. "I think we accomplished a lot tonight."

"We're not going to be dismissed. But we made some enemies."

"We already had enemies. We made the lines clear. And that we aren't going to be easily cowed."

Kitty watched her husband, wondering if anyone else was aware of just how much strategy lay behind his seemingly quixotic guest list for the evening, or the apparently effortless way he had moved about the room. "Did you declare war on the House of Lords tonight, Julien?"

"Oh, no. I'm not O'Roarke. I don't rush into lost causes. But I did stake out some positions." Julien undid his other cuff. "Malcolm's quite right that the House of Lords should be abolished. But meanwhile, the fact that I'm unelected and no one can get rid of me has its advantages." He paused a moment. "I wonder if it will make Uncle Hubert rethink the value of the House of Lords. Which would be worth it, in and of itself."

Kitty went up to him and slid her arms round him. "I love you."

He kissed her, then drew back and smiled. "I was sure we were going to get tired of saying that."

"It has a persistent ring." She reached up and threaded her fingers through his hair, then felt reality settle over her. "Tonight was only the beginning, Julien. Of a lot of things."

"Oh, yes." Julien reached for her hand and kissed it, then folded it between his own. "The next few months are going to prove very interesting."

Malcolm and Mélanie Suzanne Rannoch's adventures
in espionage and investigation continue
in Tracy Grant's new historical mystery

The Westminster Intrigue
On sale May 2021

London
October 1820

New arrivals were always a source of interest at the Chat Gris. Men were a source of potential revenue. Certainly to the women who worked the rooms above the common room, but also to the men and women who played games of dice and cards at the cracked tables or lifted a purse, a watch, a snuff box, or an embroidered handkerchief in the course of a game or while serving ale or gin or moving between the tables. Or upstairs in the rooms over the common room before or after—or even during—bedsport. New male guest were also potential rivals for the pickings on offer. Or for the women who worked the tavern. New female guests were less unlikely to come to the Chat Gris plump in the pocket, but they too might be rivals for the night's pickings, whether those were purses or watches or other trifles to be lifted or gentlemen with money to spend to be enticed upstairs. So the women who worked the Chat Gris eyed female new arrivals with suspicion. And the men who frequented the tavern surveyed them with the interest posed by novelty.

When a tall man in an olive drab greatcoat that could keep most of the denizens of the Chat Gris in funds for weeks came through the door, shaking raindrops from his beaver hat and the four capes on his coat, he drew a gaze from all round the common room. He made his way to a table in the center of the room, set down the hat, and shrugged out of the coat to reveal the high shirt points, padded shoulders, and nipped in waist affected by a dandy. They all knew the type. Sort who fancied himself daring for drinking a pint of ale in St. Giles. The newcomer with the high shirt points ordered an ale and joined a game of cards, then laughed when he lost heavily.

Several women sidled up to him, but he showed no interest, though one helped herself to his purse. He also showed no interest in three women, also new to the Chat Gris, who arrived not long after. Despite the fact that they were a striking trio—one dark, one with guinea gold ringlets, one a redhead. Their sarcenet and lustring gowns had once been fine, but any of the discerning women in the tavern could recognize hems that had been turned and lace and ribbon that had been added to cover stains and wear. That and the low-cut necks and spangled scarves said they came from a different world than the gentleman with the high shirt points, even if they were all new to the Chat Gris tonight.

The three women sauntered up to the bar and ordered gin.

Then they separated and moved about the room with the air of those going to work, something nearly every other woman in the Chat Gris recognized well. The red-headed woman attempted to the catch the eye of the man with the greatcoat but had no more luck than the Chat Gris's regulars. Then she fell into conversation with a man in a claret coat who was also new to the Chat Gris. Not long after they wandered upstairs, the man's arm draped round her shoulders and his hand slipping between the green velvet ribbons on her bodice. The dark-haired woman cast a look of annoyance at her redheaded friend, who was having better luck than she was herself, then tossed down the last of her gin and ordered another. The blonde woman was bent over the man with the high shirt points, who actually looked up and gave her a smile. Emboldened, the blonde woman dropped down on his lap.

Five seconds later, the door opened to admit another man, taller than even than the man with the high shirtpoints, though he slouched more and his swagger said he was more at home in St. Giles. He cast a look about as though in search of something. His gaze lit on the blonde woman. He pushed his way between the tables, grabbed the blonde woman's arm, and yanked her off High Shirt Points's lap.

"Take your bloody hands off my woman."

"Take your bloody hands off me." The blonde woman tugged against the new arrival's grip. "What do you think you're doing, Will?"

"I should be asking you that, witch."

"No offense meant." High Shirt Points pushed his chair back. "I had no notion—"

"He doesn't own me." The blonde woman yanked her arm from the grip of the man she called Will.

"I've spent enough on you." Will grabbed her again.

"That doesn't give you rights."

"Here now." High Shirt Points sprang to his feet. "I believe the lady asked you to leave her alone."

"Mind your own business." Will dragged the blonde woman closer.

"Julie." The dark-haired woman, who had been watching with apprehension, broke away from a stout man she'd been flirting with and ran over to the blonde woman. "You know what he's like when you set him off."

"He had no business following us," Julie said.

"How the bloody hell else am I supposed to know what you're doing?" Will dragged Julie closer. Julie pulled away from him and stumbled into the next table. When Will reached for her again, High Shirt Points stepped between them.

"Leave the lady alone, sir."

"The lady is no lady, she's a—"

High Shirt Points drew his fist back and aimed a blow at Will's jaw. A surprisingly strong blow ("Must train at Jackson's" someone murmured). Except he got his booted foot tangled in the legs of his chair and the folds of the greatcoat he'd flung over it. So he lurched into Will. Will drew his fist back to counter, but instead the two of them went down with the chair and greatcoat in a tangle of broken wood and torn wool.

"Now look what you've done," the dark-haired woman said to Julie.

"Serves him right," Julie declared, pulling her skirt out of the way to reveal silk stockings worked with clocks and cherry red satin ribbons tied round her ankles.

Will yelped.

"Oh, Will, are you hurt?" Julie flung herself down beside him.

Will put a hand to his face. "That devil fair near broke my nose."

"Poor darling." Julie looked up at a High Shirt Points. "You beast."

"See here, madam—"

"Oh, Will." Julie now had his head in her lap. She bent down and kissed him.

High shirt points stared down at them. "I suppose all's well—I say!" He clapped a hand to the side of his closely tailored coat. "My purse is gone."

"Don't look at me." Julie was smoothing Will's hair, gaze locked on Will's own.

"Julie." The dark-haired woman caught her arm. "Let's out of here."

"Not before—"

"Hunh—" Will sat up and shook his head. "Did you accuse my woman of stealing?"

"No. That is—" High Shirt Points straightened his padded shoulders. "My purse is gone. And I'm sure I had it when she sat down."

"Don't remind me that you were pawing her." Will scrambled to his feet.

"I was not—"

The dark-haired woman tugged Julie to her feet and pulled her towards the door.

"I say." High Shirt Points grabbed Julie's blue satin sash. "Don't start running off."

"Take your bloody hands off her." Will lunged at High Shirt Points. High Shirt Points blocked the blow and struck back. They lurched into the table, upending High Shirt Points's tankard of ale. The dark-haired woman dragged Julie through the crowd of interested onlookers. Julie's skirt caught on a splintery chair leg and tore. The dark-haired women pushed open the door and pulled Julie into the street. High Shirt Points lurched after them. Will grabbed him and the two of them tumbled out into the street after the women, grappling as they went, to the accompaniment of shouts and calls of encourage-ment from the onlookers.

Someone threw a tankard after them and someone else slammed the door shut on the wind and rain and mêlée.

MALCOLM RANNOCH CURSED the tight-fitting coat of his costume as he stumbled into the street. He aimed another blow at Harry Davenport, the supposed Will. Several stitches gave way in his coat, which made it easier to move. Harry hit him back as they both staggered in the mud. Mélanie and Julien had already run down the alley at the side of the Chat Gris. Malcolm pushed himself up on one hand, before he could collapse in the mud, and staggered to his feet. He and Harry stumbled into the alley after Mélanie and Julien.

The alley was darker than the street, the ground squishy with rotted food from the Chat Gris kitchen and most likely worse. Julien paused below a window, the skirt of his filmy pink gown held up, and gave an owl call good enough to have fooled Malcolm had he not been watching. An answering call sounded and then the casement window above swung open and the candle within the room caught a gleam of tawny hair. A leg clad in a silk stocking and ribboned garter swung over the sill, and with almost no sound, Kitty Mallinson let herself out the window, climbed down the upper story, and dropped into Julien's arms in a stir of green skirts and lacy petticoat.

"Good timing," she said. "I'd just secured the papers and our target is out like a doused candle. Everything go all right on your end?"

"As much like clockwork as an improvisation can." Julien steadied her and put his hands on her shoulders.

"I think we put on a good enough show that no one was thinking about what you were doing upstairs," Malcolm said.

"Thank you," Kitty said.

"Good to be back at work," Julien said. "Though I'm rather sorry I didn't get to play your part, Kitkat."

Kitty's grin flashed in the moonlight. She touched her fingers to Julien's blonde hair piece. "There's a limit to how far you could have carried the masquerade, darling, however good you are at it. And no, I didn't have to go particularly far with him before the drug took effect."

Julien grinned. "I didn't ask."

"Your husband kissed me." Harry was stripping off his side whiskers, which were coming loose in the rain. "Quite convincingly."

"I should hope it was convincing." Julien pushed his blonde ringlets back from his face. "I try not to do things that aren't convincing on a mission. Hopefully that report will throw off anyone who happened to be there or who hears about it later and remotely guesses it might have been us. My apologies to Cordelia."

"Oh, Cordy won't mind that." Harry stowed the whiskers in his pocket. "I don't think she's quite forgiven all of us for going off without her, though she claims to understand if was risky for someone not trained to fight."

"Speaking of which we should get home," Malcolm said. "Before Cordy and Laura lose patience. And before we run more risks." He looked at his own wife, who was grinning with the excitement of a successful mission. Which he admitted he couldn't but share himself. He reached for her hand. Just as three men rushed down the alley.

Harry, who was closest, knocked one to the ground first. Another rushed at Malcolm. A glancing blow to the shoulder knocked Malcolm backwards. He stumbled, then used the force of his weight to throw the attacker off balance. A third man screamed as Mélanie tossed the contents of her scent bottle in his eyes.

Malcolm glanced over his shoulder and saw that a fourth man was holding Kitty at the opposite end of the alley, a knife to her throat. Julien had gone still. Kitty fell back as though in a faint, knocked her attacker backwards and twisted away. Julien grabbed the man and yanked on his knife hand. The man screamed and the knife went flying. Julien twisted the man's arm behind his back and forced him to his knees. "Who sent you?"

Kitty snatched up the knife and tossed it to Julien. "Who sent you?" he repeated, the knife now at the man's throat.

The man made a hoarse sound. The man Malcolm had been fighting broke away and darted down the alley towards Julien and Kitty. The man Julien held slumped to the ground, a knife protruding from his chest.

The other attackers scattered. Julien dropped down beside the man who had attacked Kitty and gave a curt nod. "Gone. Damnation. I should have seen that coming. I'm getting rusty." He pushed himself to his feet and touched Kitty's arm. "You all right, Kitkat?"

"Just wounded pride because he got a jump on me."

Harry looked down at the dead man now spilling blood onto the grimy cobblestones. "Rather proving the point about needing a team versed in fighting tonight. But why the devil—"

"Explanations at home," Mélanie said.

Julien looked down at the dead man, brows drawn, eyes glassy.

"We can't move him," Malcolm said. "Or alert anyone."

"No. I know that." Julien seemed to shake himself. "Let's get home."

CHAPTER TWO

It was far from the first time Mélanie Rannoch had returned to her husband's beautiful Berkeley Square house—their beautiful Berkeley Square house, as Malcolm would be quick to say

—with a rag tag group of allies. On more than one occasion they'd encountered the watch on their return. In fact it was so familiar, she had her story ready tonight. On other occasions she or Malcolm or another of the group had been wounded. Tonight, they avoided the watch and none of them was seriously hurt, so they trudged up the steps to the fanlight and ionic portico merely wet and bedraggled.

She opened the door and ushered their friends into the entry hall just as Laura O'Roarke and Cordelia Davenport, Harry's wife, came running out of the library. "Thank goodness" Cordy said. "We were starting to worry." Then she went still, her gaze going from one of them to the other. Laura, who was just behind her, did the same.

Malcolm had a bruise beginning to form on his temple. Harry was caked with mud. Kitty's dress was torn. They were all dripping water onto the black and white marble checkerboard of the floor. But it was less their appearance that caused the reaction than what their faces betrayed, Mélanie suspected.

"No one's hurt?" Laura asked.

"Just wounded pride," Julien said.

"Come into the library and get warm," Laura said. "I'll make coffee and Cordy can pour whisky."

Mélanie set her damp cloak in front of the fire and went to the kitchen to help Laura with the coffee. It was late enough they had sent all the servants to bed, and they had all during their exile in Italy two years ago got accustomed to doing basic tasks on their own. Or reaccustomed in Mélanie's own case. She had certainly not grown up an aristocrat. Laura flashed a smile at her but said, "I won't ask questions until you can tell Cordy too. I promise."

Cordelia had supplied everyone with whisky by the time they brought the coffee to the library. Malcolm and Harry had scrubbed their faces. Julien had changed into a shirt and breeches and pulled off his blonde ringlets, though he still had traces of rouge and eye blacking. "I forgot how constricting a corset is," he said, going to take the coffee tray from Mélanie.

"Why do think I avoid one myself whenever possible?" Mélanie asked.

They settled round the fire to face the results of a mission that had seemed, as missions go, relatively simple. Gisèle, Malcolm's sister, who was undercover with the Elsinore League, a mysterious group dedicated to advancing their own interests, had reported that a League agent was buying papers from a contact at the Chat Gris. They had gone to the Chat Gris with the aim of intercepting the sale.

"And it all went quite according to plan," Kitty said, accepting a cup of coffee from Laura. "Well, as according to plan as these things ever do. The drug in his gin took effect right on schedule. I didn't even have to prevaricate. Or go particularly far. And unlike when we tried to take the papers off George Dalton in June, I found the papers right away. He didn't have dummy copies. He was still out cold when I got out the window. The others were all there."

"After staging a quite nice little fight," Harry said. "Malcolm still has an excellent right hook. Only then in the alley we encountered a real fight.'

"The League?" Cordelia asked.

"I don't see how they could have known we had the papers that quickly." Malcolm was frowning into his whisky glass. He set it down and reached for his coffee cup. "Even if their agent went upstairs the moment Kitty dropped out the window and realized the papers were gone, there's no way he—or she—could have alerted the men who attacked us."

"I was thinking the same thing," Kitty said. "It looks as though someone else knew the papers were being exchanged tonight. And was trying to intercept them."

"Just like your ball," Cordelia said.

"Just like nearly everything involving the king and queen,"

Mélanie said. The former prince regent, now George IV since his father's death at the end of January, though he had not yet been crowned, was determined to divorce his long-estranged wife Caroline. The divorce trial was to take place in the House of Lords. The Tories, as the party in power, were firmly aligned with the king. The Whigs were backing the queen, at least in part because they hoped the defeat of the bill would cause a rift between the Tories and the king and loosen the Tories' grip on power. The queen's lawyers, Henry Brougham and Thomas Denman, were aligned with the Radicals, like Malcolm and Julien. The jockeying for power and debates over the witnesses and evidence—much of it involving salacious details such as information about bedsheets—had been the talk of London for months. And the trial was just starting.

"What is in the papers?" Laura asked.

Kitty drew the packet of papers from the bodice of her gown and spread them on the sofa table. Chairs creaked and clothes rustled as everyone gathered round.

"Who's the Contessa Montalto?" Cordelia asked.

"I don't know." Malcolm looked at Julien.

"I haven't heard of her," Julien said. "Though I haven't spent that much time in Italy. Not much more than the rest of you. And I haven't heard her talked of in connection with the queen's trial."

"Nor have I," Malcolm said. "We should ask Nerezza and Sofia. But it's straining coincidence to think there isn't some connection to the trial."

"It's hard, on the surface, to see why this would be so significant," Mélanie said. "I wonder—"

She broke off as the sound of the front doorbell reverberated through the house. She took a quick glance that mantle clock, though she knew it was long past midnight. If Raoul, Laura's husband and Malcolm's father, had returned early from his trip, he'd have used his key.

Malcolm pushed himself away from the table. "I'll see who it is. At least we're all more or less presentable." He glanced at his discarded, padded shoulder coat, shook his head, and went out into the hall in his shirtsleeves. Kitty snatched up the papers and tucked them back into her bodice. Harry and Julien got to their feet. Just in case it was an attack. In general their enemies didn't ring the doorbell. But stranger things had happened.

Voices sounded in the hall, then a few moments later Malcolm returned to the library accompanied by Jeremy Roth. Roth, a Bow Street runner, had worked with them on number of cases and was now a good friend and a frequent guest in their home. But he wasn't in the habit of calling in the middle of the night. At least not for social reasons.

"I'm sorry to call so late." Roth took off his damp greatcoat and laid it on the marble library table where it wouldn't make a water mark.

"You know we don't retire early, Jeremy." Mélanie poured a cup of coffee, black as she knew he took it, and carried it over to him. "And we're entertaining friends as you can see." She didn't add explicitly that they'd been on a mission, but Roth would surely guess it. She was still wearing her spangled sarcenet gown and paste diamonds and Kitty was also still in her costume. Julien was back in a shirt and breeches but still had rouge and eye blacking on. Harry's hair was still darkened. Malcolm's high shirt points still flopped about his neck.

"I know," Malcolm said, moving back to the fire. "We've either been rehearsing a play or on a mission. Without going into details, let me say Mel is still the only one of us employed at the Tavistock."

Roth gave a faint smile, but his eyes were serious. "I was called to St. Giles this evening. To a tavern called the Chat Gris. Have you heard of it?"

"We don't generally frequent taverns in St. Giles," Malcolm said. "Except on missions."

"Yes, I know." Roth's gaze swept the room. "A man was found knifed to death in the alley beside the Chat Gris. People remembered a fight in the tavern earlier in the evening involving two men fighting over a woman and another woman who seems to have been a friend." His gaze swept the room again, obviously taking in details without lingering on any of them. "But the dead man doesn't sound like either of the men who were described. A dandy in a padded coat and a man with side whiskers and a spotted neckcloth." His gaze settled on Malcolm's coat, thrown over the back of one of the Queen Anne chairs, and then on the spotted neckcloth now hanging loose round Harry's throat.

"All right," Malcolm said, "we were there. The fight was a set up to cause distraction. We fled into the alley where we were attacked. One of the attackers killed the dead man."

Roth nodded. "To be honest I couldn't connect you with the description I got. Well, not until I saw how you were dressed. I came because I can always use your help in an investigation. Do you know why you were attacked?"

"Most likely to get the papers I'd retrieved," Kitty said. "That was the reason for the distraction. I had just dropped down from an upstairs window when we were attacked."

"You were upstairs at the Chat Gris?" Roth said.

"Retrieving the papers from another guest at the tavern," Kitty said, as coolly as though she'd been talking about meeting someone to view paintings at Somerset House rather than essentially being in a brothel.

"Was he in the room when you left?" Roth's voice was even, not shocked but intent.

"Sound asleep. Or more accurately drugged."

"Do you know his name?"

"James Blayney. At least that's the name we were given."

Roth nodded, gaze still intent. "Sandy hair, mid-thirties, wearing a claret-colored coat?"

"Yes." Kitty's brows drew together. "Was he still at the Chat Gris when you got there?"

"In a manner of speaking." Roth hesitated for a moment, as though choosing his words with care. "He's actually the reason I was called there. In addition to the dead man in the alley, we found a sandy-haired gentleman in a claret-colored coat dead in a room upstairs at the Chat Gris."

ALSO BY TRACY GRANT

Traditional Regencies

WIDOW'S GAMBIT

FRIVOLOUS PRETENCE

THE COURTING OF PHILIPPA

Lescaut Quartet

DARK ANGEL

SHORES OF DESIRE

SHADOWS OF THE HEART

RIGHTFULLY HIS

The Rannoch Fraser Mysteries

HIS SPANISH BRIDE

LONDON INTERLUDE

VIENNA WALTZ

IMPERIAL SCANDAL

THE PARIS AFFAIR

THE PARIS PLOT

BENEATH A SILENT MOON

THE BERKELEY SQUARE AFFAIR

THE MAYFAIR AFFAIR

INCIDENT IN BERKELEY SQUARE

LONDON GAMBIT

MISSION FOR A QUEEN

GILDED DECEIT

MIDWINTER INTRIGUE

THE DUKE'S GAMBIT

SECRETS OF A LADY

THE MASK OF NIGHT

THE DARLINGTON LETTERS

THE GLENISTER PAPERS

A MIDWINTER'S MASQUERADE

THE TAVISTOCK PLOT

ABOUT THE AUTHOR

Tracy Grant studied British history at Stanford University and received the Firestone Award for Excellence in Research for her honors thesis on shifting conceptions of honor in late-fifteenth-century England. She lives in the San Francisco Bay Area with her young daughter and three cats. In addition to writing, Tracy works for the Merola Opera Program, a professional training program for opera singers, pianists, and stage directors. Her real life heroine is her daughter Mélanie, who is very cooperative about Mummy's writing time. She is currently at work on her next book chronicling the adventures of Malcolm and Mélanie Suzanne Rannoch. Visit her on the Web at www.tracygrant.org

Cover photo by Kristen Loken.